KATIE BE QUIET

Darcy Tamayose

COTEAU
BOOKS
FOR KIDS

Edited by Laure Peetoom.
Cover photos: "Close-up of sheet music in book" by Glowimages / Getty Images; "Closeup of a man's hands playing a piano" by David Gilder / iStockphoto; "Young teen woman with brilliant red hair" by Eyecrave LLC / iStockphoto.
Cover montage, cover and book design by Duncan Campbell.
Printed and bound in Canada by Gauvin Press.
This book is printed on 100% recycled paper.

FSC

Recycled
Supporting responsible
use of forest resources

Cert no. SGS-COC-2624
www.fsc.org
© 1996 Forest Stewardship Council

Library and Archives Canada Cataloguing in Publication

Tamayose, Darcy
      Katie be quiet / Darcy Tamayose.
ISBN 978-1-55050-390-6
I. Title.
PS8639.A554K38 2008   JC813'.6   C2008-900242-3

10 9 8 7 6 5 4 3 2 1

COTEAU
BOOKS

2517 Victoria Ave.
Regina, Saskatchewan
Canada S4P 0T2

Available in Canada & the US from
Fitzhenry & Whiteside
195 Allstate Parkway
Markham, ON, L3R 4T8

The publisher gratefully acknowledges the financial support of its publishing program by: the Saskatchewan Arts Board, the Canada Council for the Arts, the Government of Canada through the Book Publishing Industry Development Program (BPIDP), Association for the Export of Canadian Books and the City of Regina Arts Commission.

For my daughter, Taylor Novakowski

*The dimly lit room spun around him.
John Bean knew something was terribly wrong.
He tried to reach for his cup of tea – just a sip
would do, as his mouth had become as dry as
the parchment his notes were scribbled on.
The candlelight flickered around the old
Steinway. It was time to go to bed, thought
Bean. Suddenly, he had become so very tired.
He reached for the cup and missed. All went
black as his head hammered down on the
F Key; his lifeless body slumped
at the leg of the old piano.*

John Bean was dead.

Chapter 1

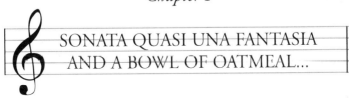

SONATA QUASI UNA FANTASIA
AND A BOWL OF OATMEAL...

Plunk, plunk, sticky plunk – IT WAS DEAD. DEAD.

The F key on the old piano was stuck again. She pulled the yellow-stained key upward with the tip of her thumb and then pressed it down again with the tip of her forefinger. Sometimes it came up by itself and sometimes it stayed stuck down. Katie released a frustrated sigh and then shuddered as she took another spoonful of oatmeal. She hated oatmeal, even when her mom at least tried to disguise the grey mush with fresh blueberries.

Katie missed her dad. With his death had come a constant ache that lived deep in her stomach. Playing the piano made her feel close to him and eased the pain. She believed that her father was near when she played. She thought she could feel his touch. Oh, and there was that voice lately – the one that kept shushing her. Maybe that was her dad. But she didn't dare tell anyone, especially her mother. It was bad enough that Katie thought she was going crazy; she didn't need her mom to think so, too.

Emma Bean rushed down the stairs, pulled her coat from the closet and grabbed her handbag. She took a quick glance in the mirror and was startled by the weariness she saw in her green eyes. The loss of her husband had left her eyes empty. She brushed her mess of short-cropped mahogany curls back with her fingers exposing the paleness of her face, and then noticed the glint of her wedding ring. Thoughts of John passed fleetingly through her head – his bespectacled unshaven face, his broad shoulders that she had always found comfort in and his easy smile.

The sound of the piano brought her back to the moment. "Katherine Constance Bean, stop playing that piano and get ready for school."

Katie hated being called Constance as much as she hated oatmeal.

"I *am* ready!" Katie played even louder.

Emma slipped on her shoes and rummaged in her purse for the car keys. She slowed for a moment as her head began to throb. "Stop pounding on that piano!"

Katie ignored her mom. She could never be quiet. There were too many questions in her head about her dad's death. There had been too many changes lately that had confused her – like the move to Chanteclaire, and her mother's abrupt personality change. With her whole life crashing down around her, the only solace she found was in her music. The more her mother told her to be quiet, she decided, the louder the music would become.

"If you don't want me to play the piano, why did you have it moved from Stoney Creek to Chanteclaire?"

The tension between Katie and her mom became thicker. As Katie became angry, her freckles blended into the red of her face. Red hair, red face – it was as if everything from the neck up was on fire.

"This old piano is worth a lot of money, even if it is flawed," Emma said. She lingered at the piano, examining the distressed patches on its surface. "We can sell it."

"You mean, *you* can sell it and make some money from it. Another thing," Katie added, "it's not *flawed*. It's – it's *familiar*, is all." Katie wondered how that word sputtered from her mouth. It was a word that her dad would have used.

Emma squeezed her way around the fan of the grand piano toward the door. "It takes up too much space."

"Doesn't." Katie noticed how tired her mother looked. She hadn't really taken a good look at Emma lately. Her dad's death seemed to have made them blind to each other. "Anyway, Dad wanted me to play."

"Don't ever be a musician," Emma said as she left the house. "You'll never make a living of it. Besides," she mumbled as her pace slowed, "your heart will break just like..." The door slammed behind her.

"Just like Dad's." Katie finished her mother's sentence.

IT WAS 7:15 IN THE MORNING. The school bus would be cornering their street soon. Katie couldn't even think about school; her mind was muddled with thoughts of her upturned life. She was furious at her mother for so many things. She hated her for moving them to her father's old home town of Chanteclaire; for making her go to this new school; and for separating her from her friends (though she wasn't even close to the few she had). But what made Katie angry the most was that her mother hadn't talked about her father since his death.

At 7:20 Katie ran her fingers over the name above middle C. "Steinway," she whispered. "A 1930s Steinway." Then she played all 88 keys, and all responded with that subtle *wild child* nature that her father said the piano possessed – all except that F key. It wasn't *wild,* it was just dead.

7:25 Katie plunked down on the F key again and again, trying to encourage it to come back up. But it didn't. Despite its dead F key and yellowed ivories, the piano was the only thing in her life that had a sensibility about it. The piano seemed like the only friend she had right now. She began to play the *Moonlight Sonata.* The F key wasn't integral, yet she missed the sound when the piece demanded it. She tried to imagine the sound of the phantom F key, just as Beethoven might have done.

I will not, she thought. I will not *Katie be quiet.* She sat, rooted on the old unbalanced piano stool – the one her father had sat on so many times – and she circled around and around. Around and around. She stared at her backpack that was bulging with new Grade Eight schoolbooks. The thought of school depressed her.

It was 7:30. The school bus left at 7:40. She didn't want to go to school today – or any day for that matter.

She didn't have any friends. She didn't have a nice teacher. She didn't have nice clothes. Her body was going through weird changes, and her emotions seemed to be all out of whack. She never saw her mom anymore, because Emma was too busy drawing up plans for Constantine's lavender farm. But the biggest problem Katie had to deal with was that she missed her dad. How was she supposed to solve that problem when they never ever talked about him? Her mom was drowning herself in her new project. And Katie? Well, she felt a sinking feeling in her stomach that just wouldn't go away.

Decrescendo, Katie thought. I'm in decrescendo.

7:40. Tick and tock. Tick and tock. There, she had missed the school bus. It's what Beethoven would have done, Katie thought. He left school at thirteen, so why couldn't she? Katie felt invisible to Emma these days; she figured her mom wouldn't even notice that she'd skipped school. Even if she did find out, Katie, sadly, didn't care.

Katie wandered down the creaky old stairs towards the stacks of boxes not yet unpacked. They hadn't brought everything from Stoney Creek, because Emma wanted to shed that old life and start anew. A lot of their belongings, mostly John Bean's, went to the Salvation Army. But even with the purging of a life, there seemed to be so much unpacking still to do. Katie searched through boxes of magazines and books; boxes of old stuffed animals; boxes of clothes waiting to be unfolded and hung in the closets of her new home; and stacks of photographs that left her joyful and teary. She looked through crates of her mom's horticultural tomes, farming texts from agriculture school, and countless sketches of garden plans stuffed disrespectfully between pages of herbology books. What a geek her mom was back then. Still is, Katie thought.

In here. Katie heard a whisper.

"What? Dad?" Katie said out loud and turned quickly.

Finally, in a box that was filled with loose hand-written compositions and her father's beloved book collection, Katie found what she was looking for: a briefcase with the initials *J.B.* stamped into the leather. Katie passed her hand over the briefcase, over its distressed-leather surface, full of scratches and scars, over the aged inflections and pockmarks of memory. It was like finding a long-lost treasure. The old briefcase that her father so loved. This old briefcase is vegetable-tanned, she remembered her father saying to her one day. How silly. Can you smell the mimosa? The sumac? he'd tease.

"Vegetable-tanned," Katie said to herself. She wished she could hear her dad say those words again. She always giggled when he blurted out his odd phraseologies – plethora of piccolos, cello-infested concert, Bolivian bassoon baboon, vegetable-tanned briefcase. But her dad always had that freakishly odd streak in him. He preferred the word *eccentric* to odd, though – and preferred the word *creative* to eccentric. Katie was sure he wouldn't appreciate the *freakish* description either.

She touched the letters that receded slightly into the leather. First she touched the *J.* Her fingers started at the top and followed the straight line of the *J*'s spine and then around the curve on the bottom of the *J.* In that *J* was her father. Then she followed the groove of the letter *B,* down, then around the two half circles of the letter. In that *B* was her father. She held the briefcase close to her chest and it smelled like her father, smelled like when he dug up that garden in the backyard of their old home last spring, smelled like dried dirt, like a dry spell. She hugged the vegetable-tanned bag for a while. The stream of early morning sun spilled softly through the basement window, washed upon her hair, now the colour of bruised strawberries. *Your hair seems to change shades with your mood,* John Bean once said to his daughter. The sunlight held her in a cocoon. Katie was engulfed in a pool of loneliness and sadness. Tears dripped on the vegetable-tanned briefcase and it too changed colour.

KATIE WENT UPSTAIRS to her room with the briefcase in her arms. She laid the bulging case on her bed and it sank into the white of the down-filled comforter. Katie flopped cross-legged beside the briefcase. The springs of the bed responded with that familiar *sproing,* like something had gone all haywire. She threw her pillows up into the corner and plumped up a pillow nest for herself. Then she clutched the handle of the briefcase and hoisted it up on top of her crossed legs. She pressed the latch. Nothing happened.

No, you don't need the key.

"What?" Katie looked around. "Great, I'm hearing voices again," she said, shaking her head.

The latch wouldn't budge and she eyed the slightly bent and scratched up keyhole that looked like it had been broken into at least a time or two before. Where was the key? It could be anywhere, it could be nowhere. Nowhere, that's where Katie thought she was. "Chanteclaire is nowhere," she said quietly.

Katie got up from her corner pillow nest and reached to her nightstand drawer. She rummaged until she found something suitable for lock picking – a hairpin. She bent the hairpin apart and poked her way around in the brief-case lock. Up, down, and all around. Shimmy to the left, then to the right. Press at the latch. Nothing happened. All she wanted to do was to look at her father's music compositions. She knew they were in there. All his orig-inals were in there. She just wanted to see his hand-writing and his scribble of notes. She wanted to see his lyrics, the words he had written for his music. If only she could see them again.

"Crap!" It had been decided several years ago in the Bean family that crap was not a swear word. "Crap, crap," Katie said to the ceiling. "Damn," she added, trying the word out. The word damn definitely was a swear word. She fell back onto her pillow nest.

"Dad, why did you do it? Why did you have to die?" She threw the briefcase to the wall. It bounced on her bed at the same time as the voice whispered, *Katie be quiet.* Katie was quiet, and she heard a click. The briefcase flap flipped open in slow motion as if by magic.

A shiver made its way up Katie's back. "Great, first I begin to hear voices, and now I'm seeing things," she said to herself. "And now I'm talking to myself too," she added.

She reached into the briefcase and pulled out the pages of sheet music. They felt good in her hands. Her father's music: "Winterland," "The Farmer Hymn," "Emma's Song" – all his familiar pieces were here in this briefcase. Katie was eager to play them on the piano (while her mother was gone, of course). Sheets and sheets fanned out from the briefcase.

But there was something else: a large, plain, sealed brown envelope. It was unmarked except for one thing, on the bottom right hand corner. As Katie looked, pencilled words began to scribble from nowhere and no one. There was a determined sound, a scratching as of a pencil on the envelope. What did the words say? Katie felt another shiver, but it cut deeper this time. Her stomach churned with fear.

...he's trying to kill me...

At least that is what Katie thought it said. The words scribbled in and out. There was something in front of the h – a flower or a doodle of some sort, or a part of the sentence too faded to read.

...he's trying to kill me....he's trying to kill me...

The words echoed in her head and chilled her to the bone. What was the doodle in front of *he's?*

...he's trying to kill me...

Then the words disappeared completely.

♩ ♩ ♩

BEETHOVEN'S "ODE TO JOY" *was played adequately, but not exquisitely. "Not the way John Bean would have played," thought the pianist as his fingers faltered. He began to strike the keys in frustration, then in rage. Memories came back to the pianist as the wind blew the lace curtains over the piano's ebony finish.*

"You should play more like John Bean," the determined father, a wealthy neurosurgeon, would tell the child. "Why didn't you inherit my touch? Why can't you play like that boy?"

John Bean was a prodigy whose touch wasn't only in his hands but in his ears. He won competitions throughout the province – from the north to the south, from the Gillespie Festival to the Kiwanis, from the Grand Juniors to the Strathcona. The piano came easily to John Bean. Not so to the child with the maddening urge to win his father's admiration. Poor, frail child, with hair so fine and white it was like gauze... he was often sent under the winding staircase without a meal if the practice did not go well. While he was in that well-visited cubby of the doctor's mansion, compositions began to come. Notes scratched on pages and pages. Also while he sat in that corner beneath the winding staircase, a hatred brewed for the boy named John Bean.

The birds outside made a commotion, and the piano player awoke from the daydream of long ago. Oh, well, enough of the memories, the pianist thought. Plenty of work to do. Cut to the quick, snippety snip.

His bloated hands fell off the piano and moved on to the boxes that were ready to be transported. House hunting, moving trucks. Moving was so much work, but there was some unfinished business that necessitated the move. He pulled down the newspaper clippings tacked up on the cork-board. Headlines that read: "Local Musician Dies Myster-iously," and "Celebrated Composer Dies in Sleep." Before he died, John Bean was being treated for a weak heart. Who knew? Poor dear. Poor heart. The clippings were layered in the box with the collection of teas. Cut to the quick, snippety snip. It was moving day. Off to the old hometown of Chanteclaire, then.

Chapter 2

AN ODD SPROING...

"I DON'T WANT HIM TO COME VISIT US." KATIE RAN up the old stairs and slammed her bedroom door. She could hear her mother's footsteps getting louder and louder. Then the door swung open.

"Your Uncle Constantine wants to make sure we've settled in to the new house. I've invited him for dinner on Saturday and that's final, Katherine Constance Bean. It's the least we can do. After all, he's eased our move to Chanteclaire, and given me a job. He's been so helpful since the death of..." Emma sat silent on the corner of her daughter's bed. It was if her mouth clamped shut whenever she talked about John Bean.

Katie felt utter disgust for her mother at that moment. "You can't even say his name, can you? What's wrong with you? His name is Dad," she hissed. "His name is John Bean! Can't you say his name anymore?" Katie's voice grew louder. "He's dead. Dead."

The bed coils *sproinged* as Emma rose and backed away from Katie. "Your Uncle Connie will be here soon. Change your attitude. I mean it, Katie."

"Or what? What kind of punishment would be worse than living in this stupid town with a mom who doesn't know how to talk to her daughter?"

Katie pulled her hands under the patchwork quilt and threw it dramatically over her head. "I don't like him. He is not my uncle. Why did you name me after him? He's a big fat ugly man!" She bit her lip, ashamed at her words. Why were these words coming out of her mouth? She clamped her mouth shut, wishing she hadn't said them.

Emma left the room quieter than when she'd entered it. She twisted the ring several times round her finger and cried as she went down the stairs.

Katie was confused and blamed the hurtful words that spouted out of her mouth on her mother. She decided it was best if she hated her mother for the moment, or maybe for a lifetime. Yeah, maybe a lifetime.

Chapter 3

THERE WAS AN OLD WOMAN...

Constantine Glitch was a big, burly man with pronounced features. His dark blue eyes pierced, in contrast to his thicket of wiry hair that had an Einsteinish look about it. His sausage fingers seemed so awkward that it was surprising he had once been a concert pianist. He had met John Bean at a symphony audition, and although John clearly surpassed Constantine's skill at the instrument, it was never an issue in their blossoming friendship. The two grew to be the best of friends.

Eventually, Constantine veered off into the hospitality business but kept his interest in the world of piano – this due to John. The two would often collaborate on musical endeavours such as concerts and musical scores for plays. But while Constantine was finding his niche in the hotel industry, John was still searching for that elusive idea, that one musical project that would put him in a comfortable financial state, comfortable enough to take care of his family. He was working on that very thing before his death,

"So, you'll be moving down from Stoney Creek as well?" Emma said, pouring a glass of ice water for Constantine.

Constantine settled in his chair and moved his plate toward himself. "It appears so, for now. I'm going to be revamping the hotel with a focus on lavender, as you know. I want to make sure it's done right. Chanteclaire is soon going to be known as the little Provence of the prairies." He waved his fork in his usual dramatic fashion. "It's nestled so idyllically in the foothills. Who wouldn't want to live here?"

"Me," Katie mumbled.

"Chanteclaire is a well-kept secret. Perfect for all my plans. Our plans," he said, winking at Emma.

Katie cringed and felt like gagging.

"I've found a house by the hotel," Constantine said, pushing his wild white hair back off his forehead. "Very old and creepy," he said with emphasis on the creepy. "Once I get settled, you'll have to come over."

"What about your piano?" Emma asked.

"I bought one here in Chanteclaire at an estate sale – a beautiful Yamaha. I donated the other to the library back in Stoney Creek."

Katie usually inhaled her mom's lasagna, but today she disrespectfully stabbed at it. She was beyond tired of the chit-chat. She watched a small spider spin a web in the old chandelier that hung above the kitchen table above Constantine's plate.

"This tastes delicious, Emma. Your homemade lasagna is the best. Oh, you know what? We need a new menu for the hotel's restaurant. You should sell me your secret lasagna recipe." Constantine cut into the layers of lasagna with anticipation.

Katie squirmed and gave Constantine a blank look. What was he trying to do? Horrified, she thought, "Does he *like* my mom? How could he? He is Dad's...*was* Dad's best friend."

Katie tore apart her crusty bread and dipped it in the balsamic vinegar. It was just the right texture to sop things up with. Flaked on the outside, and porous and soft inside. Katie had to admit, her mother was a pretty good cook. But even the bread didn't appeal to her on this day. She left it to soak.

"Constantine, one step at a time," Emma laughed. It was the first melodic laugh Katie had heard from her mom in a very long time. "You've hired me to manage the lavender farm, remember?"

"Yes, yes!" Constantine responded with enthusiasm. His sausage fingers once again pushed back his unruly hair. "How are the plans coming along?"

"Well, I was going to show them to you tomorrow at work...but..." Emma looked at Constantine like she'd just gotten a brilliant idea. "I think I'll show them to you after dinner. It'll be a good time to get your reaction."

"Ah, that will be dessert, then." Constantine brought the glass of water to his mouth. The ice cubes tumbled, splashing water on his face and down his shirt. Then he laughed a soft laugh that began to grow and roll like thunder. Katie remembered that the thing she most liked about her Uncle Constantine was his laugh. Not today.

Katie sat solemnly staring at the crust of bloated bread soaking in the balsamic vinegar. She noticed the spider begin to rappel down a filament over Constantine's plate.

Emma laughed along and gave her daughter a kick under the table. Then gave Katie a look that said, *lighten up.*

Katie kicked her back and rose from the table. "I'm just going to the washroom for a second. Not feeling well," she said with a snarl.

"Emma, I've been meaning to ask you..." Constantine paused and took a deep breath. "Well, John had been, I mean before he passed on...I mean..."

Katie heard her father's name and stopped just outside the dining room to listen.

Constantine continued. "He'd been working on something. It was special and he knew it. He called it his opera. I know he was keeping this project very quiet. I was wondering if you'd come upon it, Emma. It was going to be a surprise for you and Katie – he didn't want you to know. He kept it all in a brown envelope."

Katie wondered what her Uncle Constantine was up to.

"No, Connie, I haven't seen anything. But I haven't really dug into the boxes since the move. I just threw all of the music books and material in a couple boxes, really without much ceremony. I mean, it's just...you know," Emma said softly. "I blame the music for his death. If you want to go through the boxes, you can."

"What?" Katie said sharply as she backtracked into the room. "What? That is just stupid. Dad would have wanted me to have all his music. It's just stupid. *You're* stupid, Mom. This whole place is stupid, Chanteclaire is stupid, this house is stupid, and I don't want to call you *uncle* any more!" Katie stormed through the kitchen.

"Katie," Emma stood up and threw her napkin on her untouched lasagna. "Come back here. Katherine Constance Bean." The candles pulsed.

"Don't call me by that name ever again. Why did you call me Constance? Because of him?" *Katie be quiet,* a voice whispered and whirled around her. *Shh, Katie be quiet.* She slammed the front door so hard the glasses of water vibrated with ripples. The candles went out. The spider retreated somewhere into the sculpture of chandelier.

Emma turned to Constantine. "I'm sorry, Connie. She's hurting, and she seems to want to blame me for the death. I admit, I'm not much of a mom these days. I'm avoiding any talk of the death."

"You can't say his name, can you?"

Emma was still.

Constantine squared up his broad shoulders. "She blames you. She blames me," he sighed. "I should leave. Let's do this another time, okay?" He lumbered down the front porch stair.

"I'll see you at work tomorrow then, first thing in the morning?" he said.

"Okay."

He stopped at the bottom step. "You know, it's going to take a lot of time to get over John's death, Emma. For all of us." He took a step down the walk toward his car. "Katie needs you right now."

"Do you think this is easy?" Emma whispered ever so quietly. She twisted her ring. "Do you think this is easy?"

KATIE MARCHED DOWN THE STREET with a determined swing to her step. She didn't know where she was going. All she knew is that she wanted to get away from her house as quickly as possible, away from her life. She felt as if a volcano had erupted inside her. Tears ran down her cheeks in streams as she smeared them away with the back of her hand. She wished her dad were alive.

She'd only gone around the block, when she heard the sound of a piano. The song sounded just as Katie felt – lonely. As she approached the property, she tried to peer through the thick lilac hedges and the elms that seemed to guard the house. Through the arch of roses at the gate she saw the worn face of an old Victorian house that at one time must have been magnificent. It was unkempt – in complete disarray. But the music coming from within it gave the old building an eerie beauty. She walked slowly past the house, trying to listen to every note, and when she came near the end of the fence, she stopped and lingered. She marvelled at the blue flowers that had crept out from behind the lilac bushes. The pure blue took her right out of what she thought was her horrible life. She wanted to pluck one. She was so absorbed in admiring the beauty that she didn't notice when the piano playing stopped.

"Th-they are called Heavenly Blues. They're morning glories that have strangely taken to blooming in the evening." The woman laughed softly.

"Oh," Katie said and stepped back. She was startled from being caught in the act – even though she hadn't plucked one yet. The woman was leaning against the arch of the arbour gate. All Katie could see was her silhouette as the last of the setting sun shone from behind.

"You can help yourself to one of those if you like," the woman took a couple of steps under the arbour. She was using a cane to help her along.

"That's okay," responded Katie. "I was really just looking."

Silence.

"I like your piano playing."

"Ah. That was from *Winterreise.*"

"Schubert."

"Yes, rather dark and lonely. Aren't you a little young to know Schubert?"

"My dad played Schubert. Well, mostly Beethoven. But some Schubert."

"Your dad?"

Katie nodded. "Yeah my dad, John Bean."

Shh, said the quiet voice.

"Your dad...your dad." The old woman mumbled.

Katie felt a need to get out of this conversation and go back home. But for some reason she continued. "Do you like Beethoven?"

"Beethoven?" The old woman seemed to sit on the name for a while. "Not much." She deadheaded a few of the pale pink flowers that trellised up the arbour as she made her way down toward Katie. "These are clematis. They're the N-Nellie Moser variety," she said, as if it mattered.

Katie saw the woman's face now. She had piercing blue eyes and wore a scarf around her head. She was really rather pretty, in a plain sort of way. She seemed so fragile, with her cane and her stutter.

Katie generally didn't get into conversation with strangers, but she was lonely. She noticed the *For Sale* sign on the lawn. "Will you miss the flowers in this garden when you move?" Katie inquired. *Katie, be quiet.*

"Wh-what?" the woman said quizzically. "Oh, the sign. No, no, I just bought this house." She smiled with a kind of nervous giggle. "Th-the realtor hasn't taken the sign down yet."

"But how do you know so much about these flowers?" Katie asked, becoming braver.

"Why, that's one reason I bought this house – because of its garden. I know plants very well, you know," she said. "I do know plants very well."

Katie decided she liked this strange woman. She seemed slightly eccentric, like her father. She smiled. "You play the piano. Me too."

"I moved to Chanteclaire to take on a position at the university as a music professor. A rather absent-minded music professor," she said. "I would love to hear you p-play." The odd woman stumbled and her cane fell to the ground.

Katie picked the cane up and placed it in the woman's hands. "I'm Katie. Katie Bean."

"Oh, I'm sorry. Introductions, of course – yes," she smiled. "It's a pleasure to meet you, Katie Bean. My name is Charlotte Winston."

"Nice to meet you Charlotte," Katie said.

"Would you like a glass of iced tea? I've also got some apple pie. Have you ever had hot apple pie with rum sauce? It is my m-mother's recipe. She was a good cook. Yes, yes." Charlotte Winston became engaged in some deadheading. "Oh, I must sound like a lonely old woman."

"We all get lonely sometimes," said Katie.

"What did you say?"

"Um. Apple pie sounds good. Next time?"

"Yes, Katie B-Bean, another time," said Charlotte Winston as she plucked a Heavenly Blue. "Here, this is for you. A m-morning glory in the evening."

Katie turned back toward her home. She looked over her shoulder to see Charlotte Winston trying to pull the For Sale sign off her lawn with her hand that wasn't holding the cane. All of a sudden a cold breeze circled around Katie. *Mourning glory, mourning glory.*

$\oint \quad \oint \quad \oint$

THE CHINOOK WIND *circled the house like a predator – trying to sneak in through the old window casings and in through the door seams, snatching up any quiet it could find. The house whistled and moaned, making the hum of the composition sound even more sorrowful. His hands were gloved partially with only the fingers exposed – guiding the pencil to scratch out little black scribbles of half notes, whole notes and rests. The lump of a figure sat quietly rocking back and forth in the corner on a comfy ottoman. He pulled nervously at his earlobe, while the other hand scratched out the musical composition. Papers were fanned out all over the floor near the corner of the room, while crumpled ones clustered like popcorn balls in and near the garbage. Unopened boxes lay about the room waiting to be unpacked.*

Plan A was so easy. Pretend to be a wealthy patron of the arts. Write John Bean a letter of introduction. Offer up generous financing for him to write a score for the opera. The libretto was truly remarkable, he thought, hugging the tome of a story in his hands. But the musical score was the sticky part, which only a natural talent like John Bean could write. Then he could claim it as his own. John Bean wasn't to tell anyone about the opera. Too bad John Bean had to die just before the musical compositions were completed, though – before the opera was delivered. The timing of the plan was just a little off. But there was still Plan B. Yes. Yes. Cut to the quick, snippety snip.

"*This will never do.*" *Torn pieces of paper added more litter to the floor.* "*Once I get that music in my hands, I'll be the one receiving all the applause.*"

Chapter 4

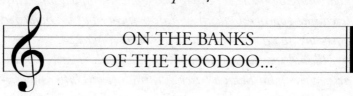

ON THE BANKS
OF THE HOODOO...

IT WAS TWO MONTHS INTO THE SCHOOL YEAR, exactly two months and one week since Katie and Emma Bean had moved to Chanteclaire. Katie still hated the town that Constantine referred to as "the best-kept secret of the prairies." *The secret is that Chanteclaire sucks,* thought Katie, as she cast a flat stone across the river.

The briefcase fit snugly under Katie's arm as she walked along the banks of the Hoodoo River. It was a calm Sunday morning. *Calm before the storm,* Katie thought as she looked up at the grey horizon beyond the coulee ridge, at the clouds that skirted the town. She wanted to steal just a bit of time by the river before going home for dinner, some time to look through her dad's music again. Katie came upon a cluster of trees that showed reds, yellows, oranges, some still retaining leaves of green. She was in awe of the fall colour. She had to admit Chanteclaire had some amazing trees, even though the town still sucked. She settled on a large smooth boulder that was canopied by an old cotton-wood.

Katie opened the flap of her father's briefcase and pulled out the brown envelope. The one with the disappearing words. She squinted at the bottom of the envelope, waiting for the words to reappear, but there was nothing. She remembered the words clearly and even remembered the way they looked – in her father's handwriting: *he's trying to kill me.* There was nothing on the envelope now. No ominous words appearing and disappearing before her eyes, and no smudge before the letter *h.* She was just about to open the envelope when a voice startled her.

"Hey! You're sitting on my rock. Isn't that my rock, guys?" the boy smirked as he addressed the other two.

Katie, go home now. The voice whispered.

Katie turned and recognized the large boy with long spiky blond hair from school. His chipped-tooth sneer became more sinister the closer he got. The other boys lagged behind him. She slid the envelope back into the briefcase.

"Yup, you're right, Snyce," said one of his buddies with a wicked laugh. "That's your rock."

"I *said* you're sitting on my rock," the boy said, standing now in front of her with his hands folded across his chest.

Katie bristled immediately, but thought it would be best to let the bully have his way and his rock. She simply wanted to go home to her room and look through the briefcase in peace. As Katie stood up and took a step, Snyce moved in front of her.

"Don't ya know how to talk?" The boy's spiky blond hair followed the tilt of his head. The other boys laughed.

Katie, be quiet. The voice whispered to no one but Katie. She tried to step around the boy. But he blocked her. Nudged her. Pushed her to the ground. The briefcase fell out of Katie's arms and from a side pocket, much to her surprise, out slid a little red book looking like a bright bull's-eye on the bed of grey stones. Katie moved toward the book as pain seared up her tailbone, but she kept her eyes on the little red book. Snyce grabbed the book, opened it up and began to read. *"The music is actually flowing today. What a surprise. I thought I'd never get through this block...* What is this?" He looked around at his buddies.

"This is crap," said Snyce. *"The music is flowing today,"* he mocked.

One of the other boys whispered, "C'mon, let's go."

"Not just yet, I think I want the briefcase," said Snyce. "Yeah, I want the briefcase."

Katie got up slowly. Her anger was rising faster than her fear. Her dad had always told her that she'd fall over and over all her life, but it was the getting up and trying again that really mattered. She wasn't so sure he was referring to this kind of situation, but his words gave her some courage nevertheless. "Give me that, loser," she said with relative calm as she brushed off her back end. *Katie, be quiet.*

"Ya know, I don't usually fight girls," snarled Snyce, "but in this case..." He pushed Katie's right shoulder.

"Give me that briefcase," Katie repeated.

"You heard her." Katie turned to see another boy she recognized from her language arts class. The one that always carried huge stacks of books in his arms. Even now, he had one in his hand.

"What're you doin' here, Noble?" said Snyce.

"Always the troublemaker, huh, Eugene? And now you're pickin' on girls."

"It's between them two, Noble," one of the goons said.

"We just want the briefcase," said the other.

"It's not yours," said Evan. "Why would you want it?"

"Just because," Snyce said with a toothy smile. "Just because."

Katie reached for the little red book, but predictably Snyce held it farther away. He began to read another passage. *"It's late and I am so tired. This last stanza is...*What the hell," Snyce squinted a bit. "Even my writing is better than this chicken scratch. *Maybe tomorrow. At least I have a title for it – 'The Wishing Well' has a ring to it..."* Snyce didn't get to finish the word as Katie's fist connected with his nose.

The other two goons backed slowly away from the situation. Their mouths dropped.

"Careful," Noble said as he eyed the boys with a smile on his face. "You're next."

Snyce crawled backwards over the river stones and gradually got up on his feet. He dabbed at the blood trickling down his nose. "We're not done," he kicked at the river rocks and pointed to Katie with a hateful look in his eyes. "We're not done." He ran down the bank of the Hoodoo River, spitting up stones behind him. The other boys caught up with him.

"You okay?" Evan Noble queried. He picked up several music sheets that had littered the area. "Here," he said squatting down beside Katie who was stuffing the briefcase with the scattered contents. "You've got a pretty good uppercut for a girl."

Katie slipped the little red book back into the side pocket of the briefcase. "Yeah, well, no thanks to you," she retorted.

"Didn't look like you needed much help," Noble quipped with a smile.

Katie began her way back home with Evan Noble at her heels. "Hey, wait."

Katie picked up her pace.

"Hey!" he stopped following after a while and watched her disappear down the walking path.

$\oint$ $\oint$ $\oint$

THE FIGURE EMERGED *from behind the row of evergreens. "Those moronic boys! She has more fire in her than all three of them put together."*

He became mesmerized by the golden rainfall of leaves, the cool air, and the autumn scent. Then a memory began to seep from the back of his brain to the front. It crept up slowly at first, and then there it was, like a creature from the night. The music filled the autumn air, wove in and out of the branches – it was all around. The sound of a nocturne, beautifully haunting, but not perfectly played. Nothing the boy played was ever perfect for his father, who was always precise, in his work as a surgeon and in his personal life. He had the perfect home on the hill, surrounded by the perfectly manicured garden, the perfect beautiful wife — and then there was the boy.

"Listen," the father would say as the Beethoven piece played over and over through the speaker system in the house, "This is how it should sound." It was unnerving to the child, how the taped piece echoed in every room. "Listen! Listen! Why can't you get this piece right? Why can't you play it like John Bean?"

The child sat at the grand piano, slumped like a wet doll. The golden leaves were cascading, falling gently, quietly, beautifully outside the large, perfect window. Then the boy played. Played to the movement of the autumn leaves, lilting, quiet. Quiet. The tears fell one by one on the keyboard like the autumn leaves — falling one by one. The father came up from behind the child, his footsteps angry, and he closed the piano lid on the boy's hands. "You're hopeless. Go to the corner until you are ready to play the piano. I mean really play the piano." The child didn't even make a sound, only grabbed the pencil from the piano ledge, the pad of foolscap paper, and went to the corner of the big, perfect house on the hill. It was on that day that the darkness fell completely upon the child — black, black, black as ebony.

Chapter 5

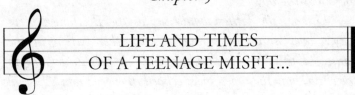

LIFE AND TIMES
OF A TEENAGE MISFIT...

KATIE WONDERED WHY THE ALARM HADN'T GONE off. It was yet another flawed beginning to yet another boring day in Chanteclaire. She wondered how depressing today would be. The concept of *today* was a question mark for Katie lately. What would happen today or the next day? She lay in bed for a while, wishing she could go back to her deep sleep, her dreams. It was really tempting, because her dreams had become better than her reality. She reluctantly slid out of bed, washed her face with one pass of the towel, and gave her teeth a couple of sweeps. She threw on a pair of jeans, rummaged through the pile of clothes on the floor for a T-shirt, and then pulled on the hoodie that hung on the doorknob.

Would life always be this stupid? Would it always be this painful and hopeless? Katie wondered these things as she ran down the stairs while pulling a brush through her thicket of red hair.

Katie noticed the note on the piano. *For breakfast, microwave some oatmeal and sprinkle with the lavender petals in the fridge for something different.* "Lavender on oatmeal?" Katie mumbled. "It had to happen sooner or later. Mom's finally lost it." She sighed.

"Oh great, I'm talking to myself again. Proof that insanity can be passed from mother to daughter." She heaved her backpack over her shoulder and gathered her textbooks off the piano. It was 7:30.

Katie stepped up into the school bus clutching her math and science books in her arms, as if they were her security blanket. Her wavy hair seemed ablaze from the sun, her large feet making pounding echoes as she walked the length of the bus. She tried not to feel intimidated as she kept her head down, occasionally glancing up through the fringe of her lashes to scan the other students. She had to admit that even though she couldn't care less about these kids, this school, or the town of Chanteclaire, getting on the bus unnerved her. It seemed like they all knew one another, and she knew no one.

She noticed Snyce in the back of the bus with his two goons at his side and she looked for a seat near the front. Unfortunately, there wasn't one, so she proceeded to the back.

"Hey, isn't that your girlfriend?" yelled one of the goons to Snyce. "The one who hit you in the fa –"

"Shut up!" Snyce said. He turned his attention to the seat in front of him, kicking it repeatedly. Amanda Pan was now the brunt of Snyce's bullying. Pan was a slim slice of a girl who looked like she could be blown away by a mild chinook.

"Amanda Panda," sang Snyce as he continued to kick the back of her seat. "Amanda Pan-duh. I'll bet your brother's name is Peter, huh? Peter Pan, get it?" Snyce laughed at his own joke and gave the back of her bus seat one last big kick.

Amanda's pencil fell out of her fingers and rolled down the aisle as the bus came to a stop at the school. While everyone else got up, she crouched down to pick it up. A big boot came down on her fingers. "Get off my hand, you idiot!" she yelled. Tears were forming in her eyes.

"Want your pencil, Amanda Panda?" Snyce and his goons laughed. Snyce caught Katie's disapproving eye and he ground his boot on Amanda's hand.

The crowd of kids moved off the bus as Katie sidled up beside Snyce. *Katie, be quiet,* she heard. But she would not listen to that voice. Instead she pushed Snyce with enough force that he fell back down on the bus bench.

Amanda picked up her pencil and rubbed her hand. Then she kicked Snyce hard in the knee.

"Getting beat up by a girl again, Eugene?" Evan Noble had gone against the outgoing flow of student bodies and now stood beside Amanda.

Snyce cast Katie a sideways glance that was filled with hatred. "Hey, Bean!"

"C'mon," Katie said to Amanda and they made their way off the bus.

"Hey, Bean," Snyce yelled from the back of the bus. "I heard your dad killed himself."

Katie winced with pain. *Katie, be quiet,* the voice soothed. She stepped off the school bus.

Katie began her school day in a daze as Snyce's cruel words dug into her heart. She went to her locker and struggled with her combination as she did every day. Then she went to sign in with her advisor, and then to her first class. The library was bustling with students from Mr. Baranski's Language Arts class and Miss P. Boyle's Science class. Mrs. Zook, the old librarian, was having a difficult time keeping the voices down on this hectic library day. She bustled her way around from table to table with the big dictionary she always kept under her arm.

"Eugene Snycer!" There was some giggling and snickering. Then Mrs. Zook, who would have made a great drill instructor in another life, slammed the book down on her desk and the library was silent. Even the teachers stood still. "Stop your antics! If I have to shush you one more time, you'll be suffering the consequences with The Big P. It's not me you have to worry about – it's the P."

"Ooo, scary."

All eyes were directed to Snyce's table.

Mrs. Zook tucked the dictionary back under her arm and rambled like an old time gunslinger toward Snyce's table. "Do you understand?" she said.

"Yessir." Snyce gave a mock salute behind her back.

She turned quickly, giving Snyce the evil eye. "What did you say, Eugene?"

"Yes, Mrs. Zook."

Satisfied, Mrs. Zook retreated to her library desk.

Snyce hissed low, "Buzzing old busybody. Shush. Yeah, whatever."

"Onomatopoeia," Evan Noble whispered in Snyce's ear as he walked past Eugene's table full of goons. "O-N-O-M-A-T-O-P-O-E-I-A, onomatopoeia. Words that reflect their sounds. Like buzz or shush."

"What did you call me, pencil head?" Snyce exploded. "Noble, ya friggin' freak!" The thought of Mrs. Zook made him immediately clamp his hand over his mouth.

Mrs. Zook squeezed Snyce's shoulder like a padded vise. "You, me, and the Big P." She promptly led Eugene Snycer to Principal Payne's office.

The library quieted.

"What are you going to do your report on?" Amanda slid into one of the empty seats at Katie's table.

Katie was glad to see her. She was feeling more lonely than usual on this day. "I'm still thinking about it," Katie replied, tilting her head sideways to read the spines of Amanda's stack of books. *Leaf and Land: A Study of North America's Natural Medicines. The Mysteries of Eastern Medicine.*

"Chinese medicines," Amanda replied. "My great-grandfather was an apothecary – a medicine man in China. That's what I'm going to do my report on. Old Chinese medicines."

"Hey, that sounds fascinating," Evan Noble said as he sat down.

"Eavesdropping?" Katie said.

"Look Bean, I wouldn't be sitting here if it wasn't for Amanda Pan. I'm her number one fan," he teased. "And the way you treated me down at the Hoodoo River on the weekend... Well, let's just say making friends is not something you excel at."

"Ouch," Katie whispered.

Amanda rolled her eyes. "Don't mind him, he's trying to impress you with his wit. He thinks it's show-time all the time."

"She's always had a soft spot in her heart for me." Evan winked at Amanda.

"Yeah, Evan's been stalking me since Grade Two."

"Stalking seems so harsh. I like to call it *being overly protective,* or even a *natural fascination.* Stalking is..." Evan's voice trailed off. He had a habit of trailing off mid-sentence. "So, Bean," Evan unloaded his back-pack and leaned toward Katie. "What is your Baranski project about? *How to Make Friends and Influence Bullies?*"

Katie sighed. "I dunno, maybe *How to Become the Most Unpopular Girl in the School,* or *The Life and Times of a Teenage Misfit.*"

Evan chuckled.

"Ya know, Bean, I could get to like you. It would take a while, but miracles do happen." Evan pushed up his glasses and began covering the table with his stacks of reference books.

"Geez, Noble, grisly," Amanda said as she scanned Evan's books. "Deviant behaviour, homicides, crime investigation. These your dad's?"

"Some are Dad's, some from the Chanteclaire Public Library."

Katie picked up some glossy black-and-white photos that had slid out of a folder. "What are these?" Katie gasped as she glimpsed the top photos of a body of a woman slumped over a kitchen table.

Evan grabbed them and put the folder into his backpack. "Whoops. Those are from my dad's office. He'd kill me if he found out I took them."

"Why do you have them?" Katie asked. She began to wonder about Evan Noble – first the reference to stalking, then the photos. Katie was getting a real creepy feeling about him.

"Don't worry, he's perfectly harmless, Katie." Amanda sensed Katie's uneasiness and her eyes bored into Evan's, as she waited for an explanation that supported her claim. "Well, Noble, explain how you are not as crazy as it may seem right now."

"I'm working on the Baranski project, okay? It's about unsolved crimes – a cold case. My subject is Opal Witherspoon."

"Opal Witherspoon, the old piano teacher?" Amanda queried. "Why would you want to do a report on her? She died peacefully in her home."

"That's what the police report said at the end of the investigation, but my dad still believes she was murdered. There were traces of an unknown substance in her system. And then there was that sketch of Beethoven under her slumped body."

"So what?" Amanda said. "She was a piano teacher."

"Yeah, but the sketch was affixed to the floor with a kitchen knife."

"Affixed, huh?"

Evan echoed Katie echoing himself. "Yeah, affixed. A-F-F..."

Amanda bit at the end of her pencil. "'Kay, here's a theory, Noble. Opal Witherspoon had a heart attack at her kitchen table. Her picture of Beethoven slipped from her hands to the floor. She slumped, the knife fell off the table and it pierced the sketch to the floor."

"Not bad," Evan said. "Plausible."

"Plausible?"

"Yeah, plausible. It means believable. P-L-A-U...'"

"Morbid subject for a Language Arts project, though," Amanda said as she opened one of her books to a picture of shark cartilage.

"Oh, and monkey toes, shark fins, rhino horns, toad eyeballs and elixir of newt are more appropriate?"

"Oh Evan, quit exaggerating. My great-grandfather's collection doesn't include elixir of newt. You're probably thinking about the lizard tails." Amanda redirected her attentions. "Have you thought about your report yet, Katie?"

"Hmmm, not sure." Katie smiled. "Speaking of Beethoven, he is my favourite composer."

"Well, there's no doubt that he fits the criterion," Amanda added, "He is old."

"Yeah, he's old as dirt," Evan said. "But can't you find your own subject matter, Bean? Beethoven plays an integral part in my report on Opal Witherspoon. What about that precious little red book of yours? Maybe you could lift an idea from that? I mean, it seems to be full of musical..."

"You don't know anything about that red book," Katie snapped.

"Hey, I'm just trying to give you some ideas so you don't have to steal mine. Why not choose Bach or Tchaikovsky?" he added.

"Trying to impress, Noble?" Amanda said.

"How about Schubert?" Evan pressed on.

Katie was silent for a while. "Yeah, my dad liked Schubert."

"Then pick Schubert to write the report on," Evan said with finality. "s-c-h-u--..."

Amanda glared at Evan. "Shut up, Noble."

"What? She said her dad likes Schubert. I mean liked."

Katie felt her stomach churn on empty and she just wanted to find a corner to curl up in and cry. She knew her father would want her to be happy. He always said that was all he ever wanted – for her to be happy. But right now she just wanted to scream at Evan Noble. Scream at the world. Because life was just not going right. Life was going wrong. *Katie, be quiet,* the voice calmed. Katie churned on in silence.

Chapter 6

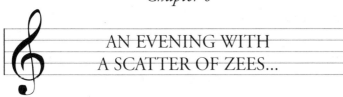

AN EVENING WITH
A SCATTER OF ZEES...

THE LIVING ROOM COFFEE TABLE WAS COVERED WITH garden sketches mounted on matte boards. Katie pulled up the onion-skinned overlay from one of the designs. LAVENDER FIELDS of CHANTECLAIRE, Katie read as she examined the five-acre garden plans. The tag line beneath read: *Provence on the Prairies.*

"Help me with this, Katie," Emma said with urgency. "Put that dishcloth down on the counter. This is hot. Ouch. Hot. Hot."

Katie quickly folded the damp cloth in a bit of a square and laid it down for her mom. "Another lasagna dinner?"

"Well, your uncle Constantine didn't get a chance to eat in comfort the last time," Emma said. "Katie, I want you to apologize to him for the way you behaved the other night, for the things you said." Emma raised an eye to Katie and poked at the foil-encased garlic toast.

"Mom," Katie huffed, "why should –"

The doorbell rang.

"They're here. Get that, will you?" Emma said as she began to angle-slice the toast.

"They?" Katie wondered as she reached for the door. An image materialized in her head. *A short, round, evil elf of a man and a prickly stick woman dressed in black and white.*

Katie opened the door wide to what appeared at first glance to be a trio of penguins.

Constantine stood, wide-eyed and wiry-haired; his large top-heavy figure held some flowers in one hand and a gift box in the other. On one side of him was a white-haired woman dressed in *haute couture* black and on the other side a plumpish man tugging nervously at his ear. The woman quickly reviewed the inside of the house, arching her left eyebrow so high that Katie thought it might get away from her.

"No paintings on the walls?" the woman blurted. "Naked."

The round man dry-coughed. "Well, what do you expect, Estelle?" He began to pull at his black leather gloves and then slid off his black leather beret. *Glabrous,* thought Katie. Shiny of head. She thought of Evan Noble and his word games.

"Hello, Katie," Constantine said with a wink.

The stick woman and plump man ushered themselves past Katie like slabs of cold meat. She felt an icy chill skim over the places on her arms where they brushed by with quick and insincere hellos.

"Emma, these are the two I was telling you about," said Constantine. "Our new head chef and restaurant manager, Mordecai W. Nightshade and Estelle Michelle.

They've just come from France, where they worked at and operated several fine establishments."

"Zees eez true," said Estelle. "Paris, Provence." Her accent came and went.

Constantine nodded. "Mordecai here was born and raised in Chanteclaire. He knew John."

"You knew my husband?" Emma said as she wiped her hands on her apron. She was eagerly waiting for an anecdote about John from the round man. But her hope disappeared as quickly as it came.

Mordecai simply nodded and gave Emma and her apron a quick up-and-down summation, disapproval clearly on his face. He caught sight of the sketches on the coffee table. "Constantine says you are an artist."

"I –" Emma began.

"You know, before we got into zee restaurant business, Mordecai and I were both in art school for zee little while," Estelle said. "We studied all zee great masters."

Mordecai nudged Estelle. "Shut up," he whispered.

"Well, yes, I like to paint," Emma continued. "But really, it's agriculture... I mean, I have a degree in agriculture."

"Surely you know that lavender fields are more than agriculture." Mordecai pressed the corners of his moustache down.

Constantine tried to lighten the mood. "They were eager to see your sketches for the lavender farm and to discuss ideas on integrating lavender into the hotel restaurant."

"Come sit down at the table," Emma said. "Dinner's ready. We can look at these proposals later."

"Sank you for inviting us to zee dinner at such short notice," Estelle said. "We are very excited to work with you and Constantine on zee project."

Katie felt invisible.

Mordecai sipped at his glass of wine. Immediately, a look of repulsion swept over his face. "Ugh, is this cooking wine?" he sputtered.

"It's a variety from the Okanagan Valley. I picked it up while on a research trip to the Mystic Ranch Lavender Farm near Kelow –"

"This reminds me, Constantine. I prefer not to stock the restaurant with domestic." Mordecai fussed at his plate of lasagna. His hands slipped quickly under the table after each bite, as if he were hiding them.

"Well, I...the wine is neither here nor..." Constantine began.

Estelle interrupted. "As I said earlier, Mordecai and I met in Paris at art school. I read his palm during zee lecture on Post-Impressionists. Oh zee poor Van Gogh, such a tragic figure, non? But zee 'Starry Night' – genius."

"Estelle!" Mordecai said.

"Yes, we met at art school. You could say we have been in a partnership ever since," said Estelle with a tone of mystery. "Mordecai's hands fascinated me."

All eyes went to Mordecai's hands as they slipped once again beneath the table.

"You're artists?" Emma asked plating her lasagna last.

"Were." Mordecai glared at Estelle.

Katie was becoming dizzy from the scattered conversation. It was like she was watching a tennis match with too many balls in play. Odd balls, she thought.

"We set up zee tea room in a sleepy hollow of Provence that became very popular," Estelle said. "I read zee palms as a side business."

"Tea room?"

"Oh yes," Estelle said. "A tea room full of all sorts of concoctions. Angel Falls for its pale blush, Linden for zee calm heart, a special Bengal spice for the nights of the mistral, all zee florals, mints, and exotics. Mordecai even made teas. He has an exceptional nose."

"Isn't that dangerous?"

"Not if you know what you're doing," Mordecai said with more than a hint of complacency.

There was silence for quite a while.

Constantine coughed a nervous cough. "Well, how wonderful! I'm surrounded by all these talented artists."

There was awkward silence. The sounds of cutlery echoed.

Constantine began again. "What did I tell you about Emma's lasagna, Mordecai? Isn't it fantastic? Shall we incorporate it into the menu?" Constantine winked at Emma.

"No," Mordecai responded sharply and sipped again at his wine. "I already have a lasagna recipe. Authentic. I found it in a little restaurant along the Mediterranean. Of course it is my Provençal adaptation of the original recipe. In any case, it is exquisite."

There was more silence.

After dinner Katie helped Emma clear the table. Coffee was served along with Emma's homemade strawberry-rhubarb crumble pie and a dollop of slightly thawed French vanilla ice cream.

"Do I have to hang around?" Katie whispered from her corner on the couch. "They're so boring and rude. I wanna go."

"Where?"

"Anywhere but here."

Emma gave Katie a look that said, "You owe me one."

Katie stayed.

"These look great, Emma," Constantine sank into the chesterfield as he lifted the overlay to one of the sketches of the lavender field.

Emma laid the other illustration boards on the coffee table. "I like this one in particular. The large restaurant window overlooks the lavender field, as do the hotel rooms that face the foothills. A stone path weaves into the lavender field leading to a Provençal-style building. This building could be used to harvest, preserve and distill laven –"

"Too busy." Mordecai cut off Emma's words. "The way the field angles around the restaurant window. Not at all what I want. These won't work."

"The designs can be modified. They are simply initial ideas to work from," Emma offered. "I gained my inspiration from Lardiers in Provence."

"Lardiers?" Estelle's interest was piqued and she studied the sketches more carefully. "I know Lardiers very well. Yes, yes, there eez the feel of zee Provençal charm."

"Don't be ridiculous," Mordecai snapped. "There is absolutely no soul of Provence in these sketches. Look at them, Estelle! How could a prairie horticulturalist possibly know anything about the lavender fields of France? You are a long way off from capturing the true feel of the south of France." Mordecai's head was turning red. "You must pretend you are blind in a lavender field first, before you can begin to understand this. Let alone sketch it. You must use your nose to develop a concept. Imagine the perfume of the lavender."

"Of course, of course." The words rolled off Estelle's tongue. "Zee nose..."

Katie noticed Estelle's left eyebrow rise, threatening to leap off her forehead again.

"No. No. No." Mordecai said.

Constantine began to cough again. He stacked the design boards and ignored Mordecai's ramblings. "Emma, these are magnificent. Can I take them home and look them over?"

Emma nodded, wondering how in the world she was going to work alongside Mordecai. He seemed so...

"Villainous?" Katie whispered in her mother's ear.

"What?" Emma looked at Katie in slight shock. "Did you read my mind?"

"Thinkin' the same thing?"

Emma nodded.

"Just a telepathic mother-daughter moment, Mom."

Emma smiled at Katie, then gave her a quizzical look.

"There really is some great work here, Emma," Constantine said with one of his winks. "Let's meet in your office tomorrow afternoon sometime to discuss the design, all right?"

"That sounds fine, Connie," Emma said.

"This sounds like zee good time for Mordecai and I, as well," Estelle said.

Katie looked at her watch. It was nine o'clock. Three hours with Mordecai and Estelle was three hours too many, she thought.

"Actually, Estelle, it might be best if Emma and I take the meeting alone this time. What about a group meeting later on tomorrow?"

Estelle bristled. "Hmfph."

"Amateurs," Mordecai whispered.

Katie's stomach ached with compassion as she watched her mother deflate. She sat herself down at the piano and began to hit the dead F key, *plunk, plunking* at the strained evening.

"Oh!" Constantine blurted. "I almost forgot. He reached for the gift box that he'd left leaning upright against the piano. "This is for you." He urged Katie to take the box.

Estelle and Mordecai hovered ominously in the background. Constantine blocked their view intentionally, trying to keep the moment semi-private.

Katie pulled at the red satin ribbon wound elegantly around the box. There wrapped in tissue was sheet music. Katie recognized her father's handwriting, his scribbled notes, immediately. She heard her mother gasp.

"As I mentioned before, John and I were working on a kind of opera. Well, really, it was mostly his creation and not mine. But I was helping with some of the lyrics, as you can see."

Katie noticed her uncle Constantine's familiar curvy *C* and mountainous *G* below her father's name.

"A mysterious client contracted John to create an opera. John was tight-lipped about it. He made me promise to keep it a secret. Well, this was the last piece of music he composed from that opera. He would have wanted you to have it, Katie."

"Katie doesn't really play the piano anymore. We're thinking about getting rid of –" Emma began.

"Not *we,* just *you,* Mom."

"Nonsense," Constantine bellowed. "You can't get rid of John's piano."

"Constantine Glitch, don't tell me what I can or can't do with this piano." Emma's voice became louder. She'd finally snapped.

"He loved this piano," Constantine said.

"His obsession with this piano killed him," Emma responded.

Katie watched her mother with curiosity. All the signs of a meltdown were there: eyes turning dark emerald green, sweat forming on her fine skin, voice lowering an octave. Katie could see why her father was always mesmerized by Emma when she was really angry. She was quite beautiful when she was angry.

"What?" Constantine threw up his arms in confusion. His hair looked even more of the mad scientist. "John died of a heart attack."

"It was because of that piano that John died." Emma heaved a sigh.

She said his name, Katie thought. Her mom finally said her dad's name. It was like the cork popped off her mother's bottled emotions. Katie smiled and ran her fingers across the title, and then across her father's signature. "'The Wishing Well,' by John Bean," whispered Katie. She laid the sheets on the piano and began to play quietly.

The house became still as Katie played her father's music. She played as if the piece was familiar to her. But it wasn't.

Constantine fell into the music and his mouth slowly turned upward into a smile as he watched Katie play. "She is a magician, just like John," he mumbled to no one in particular.

"It has the same pattern as the other pieces," Katie murmured to herself as she came to the end of the piece.
Katie, be quiet.

"There are more pieces? You found them?" Constantine popped out of the piano trance Katie had put him in. "You found them?"

"You have the rest of John Bean's opera?" Mordecai's eyes widened and for the first time that night he made eye contact with Katie. What she saw in his eyes was greed. They glistened all hungry and...glabrous...like the top of his head. And then Katie thought she saw him rubbing his crooked hands together. He had ugly hands with knobby knuckles. He saw Katie looking at his hands and he quickly slipped on his gloves.

"We must leave now," he said abruptly.

𝄞 𝄞 𝄞

EVERYONE IN CHANTECLAIRE *knew John Bean, especially those who grew up in the area. John Bean was the gawky-looking kid with the crooked teeth and bright red hair. He was the kid who would quiet a room when he played the piano, the kid who was called a genius, a prodigy. The kid to whom every piano student in Chanteclaire was compared.*

The hands hurt again. They were cold. The figure eased them into the sink filled with hot, hot water: soaked the crooked fingers, eased the tired mind. A sigh of relief came from the lips. Then a haunting song came from those lips. "Are you going to Chanteclaire? Parsley, sage, rosemary and thyme." Well, of course his mother didn't know that there was anything in the beautiful teas that he had sent her. There were many things about him that she didn't know.

For instance, she didn't know her grown child had fallen in love with the French restaurants, especially those quaint ones in Grasse; she didn't know her child was an expert botanist; she just didn't know how clever her child was. All she knew was what his father had drilled into her soft head, that her son would always be a second-rate pianist. That's what the mother knew.

There were things the son knew, too. Monkshood was used in more barbaric times to poison enemies. That's all it took. A tincture of this and a pinch of that. He knew that nightshade was toxic, too, but it was slow and ineffective. A bolder approach was necessary, double, triple the ingredients. Cut to the quick, snippety snip.

He wrapped his wet hands in a thick towel, put on his gloves and sat at the piano. He began to play "Ode to Joy."

"La-la-la-la, Katie Bean, where is your father's opera?"
He picked up a pencil and began to scratch out:
1. find that opera
2. find that opera
3. find that opera
He contemplated the list for a time, then began to play
"Ode to Joy" again. La-la-la-la, Katie Bean, where is your
father's opera?

Chapter 7

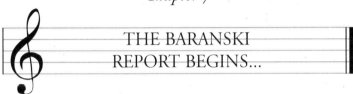

THE BARANSKI
REPORT BEGINS...

"TURN DOWN THE MUSIC!" AMANDA PAN YELLED AS she banged her fist on the bedroom wall. The sound of the electric guitar whined and twined, snaked its way even louder through the house, shaking Amanda's room. "Excuse me," Amanda swung open her bedroom door and darted down the hallway.

"Andrew," she screamed as she pounded on her brother's bedroom door. Then she leaned over the upper floor railings and yelled toward the living room, "Mom, tell Andrew to stop that noise. We're trying to do our homework!"

Katie stared quizzically out the bedroom door, listening while Amanda's screeching voice tore through the hall. "Wow," was all Katie could manage.

Evan examined the root samples and little bags of powders scattered on Amanda's bed. He reached for the magnifying glass in front of Katie.

"Yup, that's our Amanda – one moment a calm Zen master and the next a screaming banshee. All petite, delicate and fine-boned like a china doll."

"Get out of my room!" Andrew yelled from the room down the hall. Then there was the slamming of a door.

"If you don't turn down that stupid guitar, I'm going to ram it down your scrawny little throat!" Amanda's voice seemed otherworldly now. Andrew responded by turning up his amp and pounding out a screeching improvisation that made the entire house shake.

"Where was the place that Milton mentioned in his epic?" Evan tapped his nose with his forefinger as if in deep thought.

"Milton? I don't know what you're talking about."

"Ah, yes. Pandemonium," he said pushing up his glasses right above the bridge of his nose. "P-A-N-D-M-O-N-I-U-M." He turned his attentions to the medicine chest leaning against the computer desk. "Hey, look at this, Bean." Evan reached for a partially burnt photograph. "Geez, look at this guy. What an old geezer."

At that moment Amanda charged in, full of energy. "Hey, Noble, that's my great-grandpa you're calling an old geezer," she said as she shut the door behind her. "My dad would kill me if he knew I had that box of goodies in here. But I need it for my Baranski report."

"What's in it?" said Katie as she mentally counted twenty-five little compartments and twenty-five little wooden knobs.

"Stuff." Amanda opened the first little drawer in the upper left corner and unrolled the little scroll of paper in it. "This one is shark fin. It promises a long life." She pulled at the next little knob. "This one is full of...uh, I can't read it. It seems to say... Well, the English isn't too good. Looks like some kind of *love* something or other."

"Love potion?" Katie said.

"Juliet drank a love potion for Romeo. She died for Romeo. Then Romeo followed suit. True love. Any takers?" quipped Evan. "Juliet was a true romantic."

"Juliet was a loser." Amanda skipped over the title and read the rest. "Prescribed for those with a weak heart but use with caution as abuse can prove fatal."

"Well, that makes sense," Evan said. "Love can prove to be fatal. Right, Amanda Pan?"

Amanda kicked Evan without even taking her eyes off the old piece of ragged paper.

"Let me see it," Katie said as she reached for the little scroll in Amanda's hand. "I'm good at reading scribbles."

Evan rolled his eyes. "Yeah, a real clairvoyant. A Chanteclairvoyant! I'm so brilliant. C-H-A-N-T-E-C-L-A-" His voice trailed off as he noticed the girls weren't paying any attention to him.

Katie squinted and put the note to the lamp on the computer desk. "Hmm, yes, I can see the *love* written out. But there are more letters in front like *oxlove* or...wait a moment." The letters all appeared for one split second for Katie to see. And she whispered, "Foxglove." Then the letters disappeared again leaving *oxlove*. Katie saw a vision. *Hands twisting up dried leaves into a cup of hot tea.*

The sound of an electric guitar started up again with a squeal and a few sharp charges.

Amanda's face contorted again.

"Hey, let's do our reports at my house," Evan offered. "Dad won't mind. He's probably busy working on a case anyways."

Chapter 8

YOU'VE BEEN LOSING A FEW MARBLES LATELY...

GRAEME NOBLE THREW HIS OLD LEATHER JACKET on one of the hooks in the porch. He was tired and glad to see the inside of his house. But he was so hungry. He shook off his hiking boots toward the place beneath the bench. He missed having dinner ready when he came home. Missed the *How are you, honey*s and even the *It's about time you got home*s. How long had it been now? Since she left him, since she left *them* – about three years now.

"Evan," Graeme called to the living room. He flicked on some lights and made his way to the fridge. Nothing. He dialed up Queenie's. He was in the mood for some lasagna and a thick slice of buttery garlic toast. He added a large pizza to the order to tide them over for tomorrow's breakfast.

"Hey, Dad," Evan called from the porch. The three wandered into the kitchen.

"Hi, Mr. Noble," Amanda chimed. "Hope you don't mind. We're going to do our homework here. My brother was driving us crazy with his electric guitar."

"Hello, Miss Pan, whatcha got there?" Graeme smiled as he poured himself a glass of cold milk. "A medicine chest of some sort, eh?" He was a *details* kind of investigator – research-oriented, meticulous, astute, intuitive – that sort of detective. He took pride in his perceptive skills. He ran his fingertips over the small drawers. "At least a century old. Hmm, yer parents know you brought this over then, eh?"

"Well, not exactly," Amanda hemmed.

"Looks t' be Chinese elmwood, eh?" Graeme looked closer and sneezed.

"How did you know that?" Amanda propped the chest on the kitchen table as centuries-old dust puffed out from the cracks and crevices.

Graeme began to sneeze again.

"That's what he does," Evan replied with a shrug and threw his jacket over his books. "He's into antiquities. Likes old stuff."

"Hey, Dad, this is Katie Bean. She's a new kid."

"Katie Bean. There was a John Bean, I noticed in the newspapers a few months ago – Stoney Creek..." He stopped. He was tired. The words were thoughtless.

"That's my dad – *was* my dad," Katie said. She felt awkward. She was feeling like that a lot these days.

"I'm sorry," Graeme went to the sink and washed his hands. "Heard he was a very talented man." He wiped his wet hands on his jeans.

"Geez, Dad," Evan said. He was a little embarrassed. "There's a towel under the sink."

"So what's the homework tonight?" Graeme pulled a carrot from the bag in the fridge and began to chomp.

"Baranski has us all doing reports on something old. He wants us to dig up ghosts from the past. Amanda is doing hers on her great-grandpa who was a travelling medicine man in China." Evan stood between his books and his father.

"What about you, Katie?" Graeme noticed a math tome in her arms. "The ghosts of integers past?" He tried to make her smile.

"I-I'm not sure yet."

"Are there any female boxers from the past?" Evan teased. "She punched Snyce in the nose last week."

"No kidding?" Graeme Noble took another glance at the seemingly quiet girl with the fiery red mane. "No kidding? I've had several run-ins with Eugene Snycer and his little gang. I'm sure he had it coming to him, but all the same, you should take my advice and stay away from that one." Graeme turned his attention to his son. "So what about you, Evan? What's your report on, then?"

Evan was uneasy for a moment. "I'm just not sure yet," he lied. He slipped a look at his jacket that was concealing the books and the folder of photos. His hand found the marble in his pocket that he'd been fidgeting with all day. He was glad to find a diversion. "Oh, Dad, I found this for your collection." Evan handed his dad a large glass marble with a bright red plume. "I found it down by the river bottom. It's a lucky one. You've been losing a few lately and, well…"

Graeme held the glass globe up to the kitchen light, admiring its bright red swirl. "Hey thanks, Evan. I don't have one that looks like this." He threw the marble up in the air and caught it. "Well, I'm going to work in my office. I ordered some food. Lasagna for me – and you kids can share the pizza." Graeme felt the coolness of the marble in his palm as he walked down the hall.

Evan pulled his jacket off his stack of books on homicide and crime investigation and the folder of the Witherspoon photographs. All of a sudden he jumped as his dad crept up behind him.

"Oh, and I'll take those." Graeme reached for the Witherspoon photos. "You'd best find another topic for your report, son. This is grown-up work. In any case, you won't be using this as research. And I'll remind you again not to be snooping through my files. Am I clear on this?"

Evan nodded.

Graeme went back to his office. He tossed the marble up in the air and caught it. "Nice marble."

$$\text{\Large ♮ \quad ♮ \quad ♮}$$

THE CHINOOK SHOOK *the old house. Tumbleweeds scratched by the wooden siding like herds of dried up old skeletons – bristling, scraping for a place to rest from the push of the wind. Headache. Splitting headache. Get out of my house, get out of my head, he yelled to the wind. Then sat in the corner and began to sketch out notes furiously. Page after page of notes. Trying to compose something – anything.*

The thirsty tumbleweeds circled the house and gathered in a cluster in the corner of the caraganas.

The slumped figure remembered – the memories were never too far from the surface. Observe your rests, his father would insist. Observe your rests. But the suggestion didn't register with the child and he continued to play as if the piece were one long breath. For that, he was punished. Get to the corner, his father would say and drag the child by the arm, by the hand, by the fingers. Cut to the quick – snippety snip.

Soon the notation turned to words and the words turned into a plan. "Tomorrow. It all begins tomorrow."

Chapter 9

F KEYS AND LINDEN TEAS...

THE KITCHEN FLOORBOARDS CREAKED AS CHARLOTTE Winston prepared the apple pie with rum sauce. They creaked when she went to the fridge to get the pie. Creaked as she went to the microwave to heat the rum sauce. "Come," Charlotte said as she carried the plates through the living room toward the front screen door. Creak, creak as she neared the front door.

"L-let's eat on the veranda. It's warm for an October day. Th-there aren't many days left for me to enjoy this garden. There's a tree out here with fire-coloured leaves. Nearly the same shade as your hair, my dear." Charlotte proceeded outside.

"Okay," Katie said. She felt compelled to play a few chords on Charlotte's piano. She was curious about how the F key sounded in particular. She pressed. It sounded good. It wasn't a *plunk plunk* like on her father's old piano. Charlotte's F key made a perfect sound. Katie pulled the bench closer to the piano, and slid her fingers over the liquid surface. It was like the piano she'd played after her father's concert at the Stoney Creek Arts Theatre. One of the rare occasions in the last years of his life that he ever performed publicly.

But now she knew why. It was because he was so busy composing that opera – quietly in the piano room in the house in Stoney Creek. He'd shut himself out from the world for hours, sometimes days – just him and that old piano. Katie could almost feel the soul of Charlotte's piano begin to stir and she began to play parts of "The Wishing Well" from memory. *Katie, be quiet.*

An oddly sweet aroma brought Katie back to reality. She turned from the piano to see Charlotte standing with a teapot and teacups in hand.

"My dear, that was quite..."

"I'm sorry, I should have asked before playing your piano." Katie noticed that Charlotte was crying. "Are you all right?"

"Yes, yes. That piece you were playing. That song. What is it?"

"One of my father's songs. It's called 'The Wishing Well.' Um, he's written an opera... I mean to say it's one of the songs from that opera." *Katie, be quiet.* "My dad was working on it before he died. It's all stuffed away in his old briefcase." *Katie, be quiet.*

"An opera, hmmm? You must show me this briefcase some time."

Katie continued to play what she could remember of the "The Wishing Well."

"The faculty of music at the university is presenting a concert at the University Hall. Some of the brightest young musicians in this area will be performing, along with the violinist Grayson Ten-Tennant. Well, if you played and we introduced you as John Bean's daughter...why, the knowing audience would be thrilled."

Katie giggled at Charlotte's excitement. "My father played with Grayson Tennant once in Toronto." Katie took the teacups from Charlotte's hand and they walked out to the veranda together.

"Now, I knew that," Charlotte muttered. "Grayson Tennant and John Bean played in MacMillan Theatre. Well, I was witness to that performance. There was such a resounding ovation."

Katie enjoyed her pie as Charlotte told her all about the concert.

"So, is it agreed, then?" Charlotte couldn't sit still as she deadheaded some of the petunias that spilled over onto the veranda. "You-you will play one of your father's opera pieces at the concert?"

"Well, there's one called 'Emma's Song.' I could... Charlotte, I would have to practice – a lot. My mother doesn't want me to play the piano. It reminds her of my dad and right now..." *Papers flying in a whirlwind. A hurricane was blowing in her house.* Katie could see the vision in her head like a movie or some kind of dream. But she was awake.

"W-well, my dear, that is completely understandable." Charlotte took a sip of her tea. "Ah, linden tea. So good, so good. You're probably not a tea drinker, hmm?"

"No, not really," Katie said, half apologizing.

"Try it. You might like it."

"Charlotte," Katie propped herself on the wooden deck chair. "Could I practice on your piano? Maybe? I mean, if it doesn't interfere with your work. I mean, being a professor at the university, you must have to be at your piano a lot and you probably need a lot of quiet time for marking..." *Someone wearing black gloves holding "The Wishing Well."* She was not only hearing things, but seeing them as well. Now Katie really thought she was going crazy.

"Oh yes. Yes, of course. Use my piano to practice your piece for the concert. Well, that is decided then. You shall practice the pieces from your father's opera on my piano. If you like, I mean, this may sound b-bold, but I could continue to teach you in the conservatory style of piano. I could continue where your father left off with you. It's obvious you have your father's gift. It would be an honour to teach you."

Katie nodded. "I would like that, Charlotte."

Chapter 10

THE DISAPPEARING
WISHING WELL...

KATIE FELT A GLIMMER OF HOPE AS SHE WALKED down Dusty Miller Drive. The autumn sun was like a fireball dropping behind the old Hardieville schoolhouse and the chinook clouds were rimmed with a red tinge. Katie had made a couple of friends at school and now Charlotte had asked her to perform at University Hall. Although she felt jittery just thinking about playing her father's composition, she didn't feel so much an outcast now. Perhaps Chanteclaire wasn't such a terrible place to be after all. Then Katie saw the police car parked up ahead somewhere near her home. In fact, it was right in front of her house. *Katie, run.*

She began to run, thinking only about her mom.

Katie had lost her father. She couldn't lose her mother. By the time she reached the front steps of the house, she was engulfed by fear that something terrible had happened to Emma. As she opened the door, she stopped breathing for a moment. It was as if a tornado had gone through the home, leaving the sparse wall hangings tipped, drawers pulled out and papers in a mosaic on the hardwood.

"Mom!" Katie screamed. "Mom, where are you?" She slipped over the piano books that lay strewn on the floor.

"Katie!" Emma came down the stairs followed by two policemen and a man in a black leather jacket. She embraced Katie, crying at the same time. "Where were you? I thought the worst."

"I'm fine. You're okay?" Katie spun around the room. "What happened?"

The man in the black leather jacket stepped up from behind the policemen. It was Graeme Noble. "Katie, it seems someone went through your house. Lookin' for something in particular, I suspect."

"Looking for what, Mr. Noble?" Katie felt safe around Graeme Noble. "We don't own anything valuable. Do we, Mom?"

"There was some money in the breadbox that's gone. And your mother has some jewellery that's missing."

Katie felt a new fear creep into her heart.

"Well, hmm... I have some suspicions," said Graeme. "Katie mentioned something about Eugene Snycer and his gang harassing her a while ago. That bloody gang is always in some sort of trouble."

Katie nodded, thinking the same thing as Graeme. Could it have been Snyce and his gang? At least the old piano wasn't destroyed. She saw all the sheet music surrounding the piano. The only thing that didn't seem upset in the room was that gift box Uncle Constantine had given her a few nights ago. It looked untouched. Katie walked around the cushions, over the toppled piano stool, and reached for the box. She opened it and gasped. "The Wishing Well" was gone. *Concentric rings of smoke floating and fading into the ceiling.* Katie ran upstairs to her bedroom and pulled up her mattress and let out a sigh of relief. The briefcase was still there.

THERE WAS A BIT OF BUZZ at school the next day as it seemed news of the break-in at the Bean house spread quickly through the town.

"Well then, maybe Mr. Noble will discover it was Snyce and his gang of goons after all." Amanda split up her coconut bun and handed it to Katie. "Here, try this, it's delicious. It's from the Chinese bakery in Stoney Creek."

"Hey, what about me?" Evan sat back, feeling left out.

"Noble, you helped yourself to three of these at my house yesterday after school. Remember?" Amanda bit into the soft sweet bun.

"We called your house yesterday afternoon, but there was no answer. I'll bet we called while the thieves were in your house!" Evan added.

"Yeah, I went over to that piano professor's house down the street," said Katie. "Mmm, this is good."

Evan leaned forward as if in conspiracy. "I thought Snyce might be looking for revenge – after you broke his nose and all that. But Dad says that after further thought and investigation it looks more like professionals. No fingerprints. No trace. He says they tried to make it look sloppy."

"You were eavesdropping on your dad again, weren't you, Noble?" Amanda said.

"And your point is?" Evan eyeballed the last bite of Katie's coconut bun.

"They took my dad's sheet music." Katie licked the coconut residue from her fingers and sipped the last of her juice box. "Creepy, huh?"

"Aren't you scared?" Amanda said as the three finished up their lunches.

"Well yeah, I'm creeped out. But my uncle Constantine arranged for an alarm system to be installed today. And Mr. Noble..."

"Detective Noble," Evan corrected.

"Well, the Chanteclaire police are going to be watching our house for the next couple of days." Katie swung her legs over the cafeteria bench and reached for her books, backpack and the old briefcase.

"What's that?" Evan said.

"The subject of my Baranski report. I took your advice. I'm going to write my report about my father's opera, this vegetable-tanned briefcase and the little red book."

"Vegetable-tanned?" Amanda queried. "That's weird."

"Weird like frog legs and turtle eggs?" Evan quipped.

"No, weird like you." Amanda slung her backpack over her shoulders, gathered her research books and notes on Chinese medicines.

♭ ♭ ♭

HE IMPROVISED A MELODY *on the piano, then began to tell a story.*

Her name was Opal Witherspoon. One Christmas, Opal Witherspoon received a gift from her son, whom she hadn't seen in many years. The package came all the way from Paris. Little packets of teas wrapped in special ribbons and papers. Over the winter, Opal Witherspoon tried the packet of purple teas first. On the packets was a watercolour painting of a double-bloom Japanese Iris that read "Winter Serenity" across the bottom. It was wrapped in a fine satin ribbon the colour of deep purple – so dark was the purple that it was very nearly black.

These teas seemed to put Opal in a dreamlike state, but winter always made her feel this way. Then in the spring she tried the teas wrapped in packets of painted ostrich ferns and baby's breath. These pale green teas were called "Spring Grace." In May, Opal began to have dizzy spells accompanied by hallucinations – which she attributed to her imagination, which seemed to be getting more vivid by the day. In the summer she sipped "Summer Joy." The pink teas with the Wild Rose paintings – her son must have known that roses were her favourites.

Come August, Opal began to have trouble with her breathing, and she was vomiting after extended bouts of migraine attacks. She thought that if she started taking walks in the coulees the fresh air and exercise would do her good. But all they did was make her even more breathless and confused. The autumn air in Chanteclaire seemed to soothe Opal's mind and body. She was having better days, and like her morning glories, she seemed to thrive in the cool of autumn. She was now down to her last packets of tea. A blue affair with little tiny hooded blooms the colour of cerulean painted on a mountain slope backdrop. Below the painting, as with the others, was a calligraphied seasonal name – "Autumn's Calm." Opal drank all of the fall teas, and one cool morning late in October – the month of the opal gemstone – she slumped into her kitchen chair after a breakfast of toasted English muffins topped with grape jelly, a slice of Indian River grapefruit that she'd halved with her kitchen knife, a bowl of oatmeal sprinkled with brown sugar, and a cup of delicate "Autumn's Calm." Opal Witherspoon held the picture of Beethoven her son had sent along with the tea. She hummed the "Ode to Joy," took one last breath and died of respiratory failure. Just like that. Cut to the quick, snippety snip.

Chapter 11

FILLING IN THE BLANK WALL...

THERE WAS ONLY ONE BLANK WALL IN THEIR HOME. All the rest were covered with paintings and framed antique perfume bottles of the French variety. Estelle held John Bean's sheet music, entitled "The Wishing Well" up against that one blank wall of their newly acquired Victorian house and was disappointed at the lack of impact it had on her. "I really don't know why you wanted to steal it. Really, Mordecai, what a terrible risk to steal something so worthless." She laid the music on Mordecai's Bösendorfer. "And the mess you made in zee house. *A semer la pagaille* – so amateur."

"Well, that is the beauty. It appeared to be such an amateur burglary that they'd never suspect a professional." Mordecai ran his knobby, veined hands across the Macassar ebony and could almost feel the value of the piano with the touch. He played a little of John Bean's "The Wishing Well." The sound was so fine, with just the striking of those few chords, that he was immediately soothed. He sunk into his favourite leather chair, kicked Estelle's meticulously groomed poodle off the ottoman and dug his heels into its tufts.

"I needed some sheet music to play on my new acquisition." He blew smoke toward the magnificent piano. "We're both bored here, can't you see?" Mordecai took a long drag of his cigar and watched the smoke rings swallow up the ceiling. "Just a little caper here and there to wean me off, Estelle."

Estelle cuddled the white ball of a creature into her long spindly spider arms. "Oh Coco, is zee Daddy being zee big meanie?" The dog responded with a short, high-pitched woof. "Ee duz not reemembair zee promees."

"What promise?" Mordecai glared at her. "Oh yes, now I remember. The promise to start a new life here in Chanteclaire, where no one knows about our past. Yes, I know. But you don't understand. John Bean is a great composer. A great dead composer. You know better than anyone how valuable these sheets of music could be in several years. It was the entire score of the opera that I was looking for. Where could that little brat have put it?"

"You want zee opera for your own foolish reasons — not as an investment in zee future. Stealing from the Bean girl, her father's opera? Why? The music from a lesser-known composer named John Bean. Pooh!" Estelle waved one of her arms while the other held her poodle.

"You know, Estelle, when I was growing up, there was only one famous kid in this town, and his name was John Bean. John Bean was Chanteclaire's golden boy, and every other child in town was envious. He went international, won top prizes at the Oberlin in Italy, Leeds in Great Britain, the Tchaikovsky in Moscow. He won a scholarship to the Royal Conservatory of Music in Toronto, played with all the great composers. Then he burnt out and everyone watched this piano prodigy spiral down, down into seclusion. Everyone wondered when John Bean would emerge from his dark cocoon and allow his genius to thrive once again. This opera would have been his magnum opus. Don't you see? It was such an undertaking that it killed him. And I want it for myself."

Mordecai pressed the remnants of his cigar into the Swarovski crystal dish and watched as the embers faded and the smoke disintegrated into the air. "I want it."

"Was eet zah opera zat killed heem?" Estelle whispered in Coco's ear. "Or vas eet somesing elze?"

"What did you say?" Mordecai leaned his globe of a head forward and got out of the chair.

"Nothing," Estelle said as the arch of her finely pencilled right eyebrow rose frighteningly high and hung up there for a long time.

"Where are my gloves?" Mordecai threw on his jacket. "I'm going to the restaurant to meet with Constantine about the menu, and maybe that Emma Bean will be there. Maybe I can find a way to get back into her house without suspicion – without breaking into it. Just let me have my fun, Estelle. Just this one last heist."

"Heist? Don't make me laugh. You are stealing from a little girl. This is not a heist. Ha, ha, you make zee Coco and I laugh."

"Nevertheless," Mordecai snuggled his sausage fingers into his leather gloves until they stretched taut. "And knock off the accent. You're driving me – how you say? – crazy. We both bloody well know you were born and raised in Moose Jaw, Saskatchewan."

Estelle bent down to kiss Coco with her thin lipsticked mouth. "You vould sink zat John Bean opera vas zee Crown Jewels of England or somesing," she mumbled with irritation. "He vill get us into trouble eef he isn't careful."

Coco woofed in response.

Chapter 12

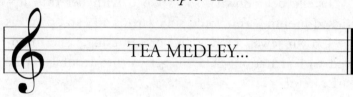

TEA MEDLEY...

"C'MON KATIE, READ SOME OF IT TO US," AMANDA said as she pulled her satiny flow of hair into a ponytail.
"Okay, okay, I'll read a little from it."

"My mysterious client has sent me a wooden crate full of teas that will certainly last the year. Teas in hand-painted packets. Imagine someone going to the trouble of painting garden flowers on the packets. They are like little works of art complete with an artist's signature – a little treble clef is stamped on the bottom corner of each tea bag."

Katie leaned back into the corner of her bed where the pillows were piled high.
"Well?" Evan said. "Read some more."
Katie continued to read from her father's red book.

"I am baffled as to why the anonymity of my client

is of such importance, but the advances are so gen-
erous that I'm not going to challenge the secrecy. I
can now support Emma and Katie easily without
looking for outside work. This whole financial
arrangement is allowing me the luxury to concen-
trate solely on composing. With my mind free from
financial worry, I've been able to focus on creating
some of my best work to date. Connie has been over
Sundays working on lyrics with me. He doesn't
know the whole story behind this opera. It's supposed
to remain a secret and so it shall for now."

Katie closed the little red book. It felt good to read words that her father had written.

"There is something very intriguing about reading someone else's diary, isn't there?" Evan said.

Amanda rolled back on her stomach and reached for her backpack. "It's called snooping," she responded. "I found some more of my great-grandfather's tinctures and medicinal herbs. It seems he was known for making teas from herb combinations." She pulled out a paper bag. Within it were small glass bottles individually wrapped in paper towels. "These have practically disintegrated over the years and the Chinese characters have nearly faded from the labels." She held one of the bags in the palm of her hand.

"Popo, my grandma, says that in China tea was dis-covered when an emperor..." Amanda looked through her binder, leafing through notes. "An emperor named...oh here it is. An emperor named Shen Nung had some leaves fall from a tree into his boiling water. He drank it and thought it tasted really good. Popo says that's how tea drinking began in China."

"So what is in that bottle?" Katie said scrunching up her nose. "It looks so dusty in there."

Amanda unscrewed the lid and read the masking tape on the underside. "This is mugwort. It's supposed to treat pain and sleepwalking. It can lead to poisoning if too much is taken."

"Poisoning?" Katie thought back to her father's red book and the tea packets he received from the mysterious client.

"Well, Bean, you should sleep well then tonight, because the mugwort dust is sprinkling all over your bed," said Evan with a snicker.

Amanda and Katie began to shake the dust off the blanket.

"It's funny, but while you two were talking about your Baranski reports I was thinking."

"Gee, Noble, hope you didn't hurt yourself," Katie said with feigned concern and pulled the corner of her blanket across the bed.

"Ha ha," Evan responded. "I was thinking that it was a coincidence that both your reports have the subject of tea in them, because mine does too. It seems that Opal Witherspoon loved teas. My dad said that when they investigated her death, there were teas piled high in her pantry and a collection of teapots displayed on a shelf. The house was filled with various tea paraphernalia. P-A-R-A-P-H-E-R-N-A-L-I-A. It means personal stuff or equipment, like you'd need for a tea collection obsession." Evan pulled out a folder from his backpack.

"Evan, didn't your dad tell you..." Amanda bit at her hangnail.

"Yeah, I know. He told me to find another subject. Look, Amanda, he knows better than any one that a good investigator will pursue a case if he has a gut instinct."

"This isn't exactly a case, Sherlock. It's a Grade Eight Language Arts report that is going to get your dad in trouble if you use some of those photos."

"I won't use the photos. They're strictly research materials." Evan pulled out two large 8.5" x 11" glossy black-and-white photograph. "This is the Opal Witherspoon crime scene."

"The old lady died of natural causes, Noble." Amanda bit grotesquely at her hangnail.

"So they say. "

Amanda and Katie looked at the photo that showed Opal Witherspoon's kitchen. It had different shapes and sizes of teapots in every corner, on the counters and even lined up on a wall shelf. "So? She was obsessed with tea," said Katie, thinking about her father's diary and his entry about the gift of teas from the mysterious client. "Lots of people enjoy tea."

"Yeah, I know," he said, handing Katie the other two photographs. "These are photos of some kind of framed tea packet collection. She was no ordinary tea lover, she was crazy as a – well, as my dad would politely say, Opal Witherspoon just needed a little re-cobblin'. What do you think of that word, *cobble?* Say it out loud, it sounds funny. Cobble, cobble."

Katie got a chill up her back that spread across her arms. *Katie, be quiet.*

"What is it?" Amanda said, taking a break from her hangnail.

"There's something right here." Katie pointed to one of the tea bags in the photo.

"Where?" Evan said. "That's just a smudge."

"That's no smudge. Come on."

Amanda and Evan followed Katie to the extra room that was being used as Emma's office. It was filled with stacks of horticulture books and art supplies. Pens and pencils, artboards and paints, preliminary sketches of Constantine's lavender farm on the walls. Katie pulled open the drawer beneath the light table and retrieved a photographer's magnifying loupe. She laid Evan's photo-graph of Opal Witherspoon's framed tea bags on the light table.

"That's no smudge," Katie whispered holding the magnifying loop over the tea bag photo.

"Yeah," Evan said squinting at the enlarged tea bag corner. "That's not a smudge. It's a treble clef, a signature just like the one your father described in his diary."

$$\text{\clef\ \clef\ \clef}$$

THE FIGURE SAT QUIETLY IN THE DARK. *The one candle flickered as wind seeped in through the door crevices. It had been a long, bleak day and the sunken comfort of the armchair was a respite. Knotty fingers dug into the tufted cushion and down the sides of the worn leather. At first, the leather was cool on his fingers, then warm. There was a memory from childhood that evoked a similar sensation. Oh yes, it was the one time, the only time, that the child's father had held the boy's hands and kissed them. It was the one time, the only time, that the child had brought home an award from a piano festival. The father's kiss on the child's hands – cool at first, then warm.*

His eyes became wet. He rose to get a coat. There was something that had to be done. Coat on. Scarf on. Hat on. The candle licked at the black air in streaks of orange. Spit on the fingers, then pinch out the flame tip. Cut to the quick, snippety snip.

He walked down the quiet streets of Chanteclaire. In an old district where the streets ribboned up and down, where lawns were blanketed in golden leaves and the bared elms arched gracefully over the boulevards, there was the old house surrounded by the neatly trimmed hedge. Manicured just as it had been many years ago.

"Are you going to Chanteclaire Fair? Parsley, sage, rosemary and thyme." There was no more time. He cinched the scarf, trying to keep out the biting gusts. The sky held little pinpricks of stars in between patches of dark purple cloud. He smeared his tears into the scarf and walked even closer to the house – close enough to see the child playing the piano. Close enough to see the father become angry. Close enough to see the keyboard lid come down upon the boy's fingers. Close enough to see the child cry. Close enough to see the child with the shock of white hair in the corner, composing sheet after

sheet, string after string of little black notes. A dog barked in the background and the strange man was shaken from the dream. The house didn't have a piano, nor a child. The sheer of snow on the ground glistened beneath the crescent moon as the mysterious figure walked away from the old house. It was time to paint. Sip on some hot tea and do some painting. Yes. Yes.

Chapter 13

OUR LITTLE SECRET...

"T-TEA?"

"No, thank you," Katie said, preoccupied with the smooth finish of the pitch-black piano.

"Go ahead." Charlotte waved her hand toward the piano and set her cane on the end table stacked with papers. "Practice your concert piece. I'll just work on these projects. There are some very good students in my group, but this assignment will show which ones really shine." She put on a pair of half-moon reading glasses and began to mark.

Katie pulled the sheet music for "Emma's Song" from her backpack.

"I was thinking, Charlotte – maybe I should tell my mom that I'm spending time here after school, practicing for the university concert. We haven't been getting along very well since my father's death, and it seems like this is just another one of those things driving us apart from one another."

"Oh n-no, you mustn't tell. Let's keep this a surprise until the night of the concert." Charlotte looked up above the rims of her glasses at Katie. "Agreed?"

Although Katie felt a little uncomfortable with the decision, she nodded and began to play.

Chapter 14

THE LAVENDER TEA ROOM...

"Entrez, s'il vous plaît." ESTELLE DREW THE DARK purple curtain back for Emma as the velvety softness brushed the side of her face. "Welcome to zee Lavender Tea Room. Well, the entrance to the restaurant, anyways."

Emma couldn't believe her eyes. Estelle had transformed the entrance into a museum overnight. Her eyes were wide and her smile grew. "What?" was all that Emma could manage. "How?"

"You like this, Emma Bean?" Estelle said with an uncharacteristic small smile. "Not even Mordecai has seen this. It's modest, really."

"You call this modest?" Emma looked around at the beautiful reproductions of the masters: Cézanne, Rembrandt, Carravagio, Vermeer. She gazed wide-eyed in Estelle's direction.

Estelle shrugged her shoulders. "Copies of zee masters are so easily accessible in Europe. Don't they have an old-world charm and an air of originality about them, though? That's what living in France will do. It will give you a style that you cannot possibly get here in a small town. You have no style because of your geography, Emma Bean. I am so sorry, but this is too true, *non? C'est comme ça.*" Estelle shrugged sympathetically, as if Emma had a terminal disease.

Emma forced a smile, trying desperately to maintain her calm. She tried to divert herself from her agitation with Estelle by taking in the replica of the antique map near the cloakroom. She sat at the leather bench and opened her notebook on the coffee table. There was faint music in the background that made her feel like she was in a church. It was all so very confusing.

"So, let's do a bit of brainstorming, Estelle."

"Okay. *Oui.* Me first."

"Okay, you first."

"Zee palm reading."

"Palm reading?"

Estelle reached for Emma's right hand and held it in hers, palm up. "You have a sure hand, Emma Bean. This is a working hand. A smart, but stubborn hand. Oh, look at all these lines. *Mon dieu,* what a mess."

Emma pulled her hand back. "Are you sure you know how to read palms?"

"Of course. Do you question my ability?"

Emma sighed. "No, but let's discuss the possibilities of lavender products. Connie would like to see what lavender ideas we can come up with. Palm reading can wait for another time. Deal?"

Estelle nodded. "Yes, you are right. But I was thinking palm reading could be a novelty for zee restaurant."

"Sure. But for now let's talk about the lavender. Lavender jams, lavender mints," Emma said.

"What about zee lavender dressing? My favourite café in Provence served an exquisite lavender salad dressing."

"Yes." Emma began taking notes despite the poor lighting. "What about soaps and bath salts?"

Emma lifted her portfolio of garden designs to the table. "Constantine had an idea to integrate one of the sketches into a logo and some labels for..." Emma's portfolio knocked against something beside her.

"Oh no, zee Stradivarius!" Estelle screeched.

At that moment Mordecai came out of nowhere and caught the violin as it tumbled mid-air. "Estelle," he spit out. "What is all of this?" His jaw clenched as he spoke. "This is not the way we wanted to design the restaurant. We really must confer!" He acknowledged Emma with a nervous smile and then cast Estelle a contrasting furtive look.

"I'll have to find a safer place to display zee violin," Estelle said with a rather ugly giggle.

Emma pulled her chair closer to the table. "Did you say Stradivarius?"

Mordecai rolled his eyes. "Estelle likes to refer to her grandfather's old violin as a Stradivarius. It's pretentious, I know." He winked at Emma. "But it's endearing. Of course it isn't a real Stradivarius, Emma Bean. Don't be ridiculous. Now, would you excuse us for a moment?" Mordecai pulled Estelle urgently aside and the two began a hissed conversation.

"Are you crazy, Estelle?"

"What? She'll never know. No one in this town will ever know that these aren't replicas, that they're the real thing. Mordecai – we've done such a brilliant job of reproducing and replacing art that no one suspects at all! Not even the original owners know what we've done. But we know. Can't it be our reward for all those years at art school?"

"No. These paintings all come down immediately, do you understand? And the Stradivarius! Our most prized acquisition! Have you forgotten the risk we took? How could you, Estelle?" he whispered. "Take these down. I have an idea of my own for this entrance and it will look nothing like all this!" Mordecai waved his arms around the room. "And another thing Estelle, kill the Gregorian chants, will you? You know how that music unnerves me."

Mordecai and Estelle composed themselves and rejoined Emma.

Emma sensed some tension between the two of them, but really she couldn't tell if it was tension or just that perpetual sinister air that seemed to always hang about them. Even in the room of calming lavender and rich ambience, these two still seemed strained.

"Shall we talk about lavender again? " Emma offered. "By the way, Mordecai, Estelle has really transformed the entrance to the Lavender Tea Room."

"Of course, of course. Now, let's carry on with discussion of lavender products and not decor," said Mordecai as the beads of sweat bubbled across his brow. "I have just explained to Estelle that this is not the look we want. These reproductions of Old Masters, the antiques, they're way too stuffy. Something with a fresh look is what we really need. Uh, fresh like..." Mordecai wrung his hands. "Like fresh lavender. Yes, fresh like lavender. Let's get back to topic, shall we? In France, the lavender fills the fields. The fragrance calms the senses and when added to tea is faintly sweet. So the lavender tea will be an important part of this restaurant."

"We are going to put zee drop of lavender oil into each sugar cube. This was my idea," Estelle said proudly.

"Now here is my idea," Mordecai said. "The French love lavender so much that they send the lambs into the lavender fields."

"Why?" Emma asked, wondering where the point of the meeting had gone.

"There's an exquisite flavour to lamb that has been fed upon lavender," Mordecai said, eager to display his knowledge. "Of course, we will also be serving lamb in the restaurant that has been grazed in fields of lavender," His tension was easing, perhaps from the talk of lavender. "I want lambs in the lavender field for the restaurant patrons to see while they are dining."

"That sounds a little too complicated for our lavender farm, but nevertheless..."

"Complicated?" Mordecai's face began to turn red again. "You don't know the first thing about running a lavender farm, and you're telling me what is complicated?"

"Darling, your heart. Let's hear what zee Emma Bean has to offer up for suggestions."

"Well, I'll leave the restaurant to you, Mordecai. The lambs in the field? That will be up to Connie. But we obviously need to harvest and process the lavender. We could start a small cottage industry of lavender products and eventually sell products on-line. Perhaps expand into a spa later on. I've been in contact with a former agriculture classmate who now lives in the south of France near Grasse, and –"

"Wait, wait." Mordecai wasn't about to take any advice from Emma or her friend from Grasse. But he didn't want to alienate her completely. "Of course we will need to create some products, Emma. What a fantastic idea. You know, you have some wonderful ideas, Emma. Would you like to get together and further discuss the lavender farm's future?"

"I suppose."

"Very well. What about at your place again? Perhaps your daughter Katie would like to play the piano for us – an encore."

Emma bristled when Katie's name rolled off of Mordecai's tongue. "Well, I can tell you point-blank that Katie won't be playing the piano for you, Mordecai, for many reasons that I don't want to get into." Emma became cautious. "But yes, if you would like to come over to discuss more marketing strategy for the lavender venture, then of course."

The corners of Mordecai's mouth curled up slowly. "Good, then, Constantine will be happy to hear that we are well on our way to developing an amazing lavender campaign. I see you are fully capable, Emma." The compliment came out of Mordecai's mouth with difficulty.

And I am aware that I shouldn't trust you for some reason, Mordecai W. Nightshade, thought Emma. At that moment she felt *a gentle caress* engulf her. "John?" she whispered looking around. There was *nothing*. But the *nothing* felt so good.

"What did you say?" Estelle said.

"Oh...nothing." Emma said as she disappeared under the heavy velvet that draped the arched entrance of the Lavender Tea Room.

Chapter 15

CROSSING THE TEAS...

"No, REALLY, DAD, THIS IS SOMETHING THAT MIGHT help with that cold case." Evan continued to follow his father around the house with the Opal Witherspoon glossies.

"Cold case." Finally Graeme Noble stopped in his tracks. "What did I tell you about diggin' into my files?" He snapped the folder of photos out of Evan's hands. "This isn't fodder for a school report. This is important evidence from a case that is dead. Property of the Chanteclaire Police Department, entrusted into my hands. What do you think would happen if the Police Chief or even the Mayor found out that evidence from a murder case was being turned into a Grade Eight Language Arts report?"

"But Dad, just listen to me."

"Look, Evan, I can appreciate your enthusiasm about your report, but this could lead to some serious consequences for me at the station. I am rather flattered, ya know, that you're interested in my work. Really I am. But…"

Evan removed his glasses, revealing intensely blue eyes, the same colour as his mother's. He waved the magnifying glass one last time. "Just take a look at this one thing, will you, Dad?"

Graeme shook his head. "Show me, then."

They went to Graeme's office at the end of the dark hall, in the older part of the house where the wind seemed to make its way through the supports. Evan flicked on the desk lamp and laid out the Witherspoon black-and-whites.

Evan began to explain the entries from John Bean's red book. "Before Katie's dad died, John Bean received teas from his mysterious client and on the bottom of those tea bags was an insignia. A kind of artist's signature of a treble clef."

Graeme Noble was becoming impatient.

"Look here." Evan held the magnifying glass over the photograph of Opal Witherspoon's tea collection.

Graeme could clearly see the swirl. "It's a treble clef."

"Dad, I think that Opal Witherspoon and John Bean were both tea-poisoned by the same person."

$$\text{\clef \clef \clef}$$

HIS FATHER *was a man who liked things done right. Meticulous and just right. Early on in his career, he was sued for malpractice. Of course, the patient who did the suing had every right. After performing the appendectomy, the young Dr. Elmer Witherspoon sewed the patient up (ever so precisely, as was his nature), not knowing that he'd left a few of the operating instruments in the patient's belly. Well, that incident changed Dr. Witherspoon's meticulous life to a meticulous, meticulous life. Cross all your t's and dot all your i's, he would say to his son, and then you must cut to the quick, snippety snip. When playing the piano, the child studied the notes carefully; when climbing the Rockies with his father, he would dig the crampons in at just the right spot at just the right depth. Mountain climbing was for the meticulous, too.*

Chapter 16

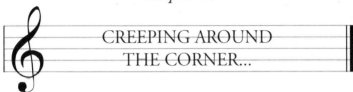

CREEPING AROUND
THE CORNER...

"To make zee lavender tea you must add zee two pinches."

"Two what?" Katie asked as she passed the cubes of lavender-laced sugar to Evan and Amanda.

"Two pinches of dried lavender," Mordecai explained, smelling, licking, then lighting and rolling his cigar. "You don't mind, do you?" he asked in Emma's direction.

"I do mind, actually."

Mordecai pretended not to hear.

"Make sure zee water is verrry, verrry hot. Do you understand? It must be hot. Hot. HOT. *Comprenez-vous?*" Estelle's r's were rolling around in every corner of the Bean kitchen. "Not boiling, but very hot. Now, let this sit for ten minutes, zen we strain zee tea."

"No, we strain carrying this box." Amanda lifted a corner of the cardboard box. "C'mon guys, let's go work on our Baranski reports."

"The box," Evan sighed. "The stupid box."

"Got it?" said Amanda, grunting a little.

Katie added her books and Amanda's to the stack Evan was carrying. "Got it," she said, lifting the other side of the box.

The top of the cardboard box flapped open, exposing the Chinese medicine chest.

Mordecai began to cough on his own cigar smoke as his keen nose smelled something other than the cigar, something other than the scent of lavender. While living in Provence, where the sense of smell is an art, Mordecai had learned the value of a highly educated nose. And now he sniffed out something of fine value.

"What is that box made of?" Mordecai sniffed, trying to pick up the scent. "Chinese elmwood?" He waved his cigar, drawing smoky curls in the air.

The children ignored him and went upstairs. Amanda and Katie carried the box while Evan did a balancing act with the books.

Mordicai redirected his attentions to the kitchen conversation where Estelle was chit-chatting about the Provençal tanneries and their use of aromatics.

"What about briefcases?" Emma asked, remembering John's affection for his old briefcase. "Did they make vegetable-tanned briefcases in Grasse?"

Estelle shrugged her shoulders.

Mordecai disregarded her query as well and waved his cigar as stray ashes floated to the kitchen linoleum like grey confetti. "The interior of the Lavender Tea Room will be reminiscent of all that we remember in

Provence. The windows will open, to allow circulation of the purity of the chinook, a cheap imitation, of course, of the mistral of southern France. We will be making our sweet cakes from lavender and caster sugar. I'll seal up a sachet of lavender flowers with the sugar for a month or so and then use the sugar as an ingredient in our coffee cakes. Oh, and I have an incredible pineapple and coconut loaf that will be irresistible when baked with the lavender sugar."

Emma began to cough while she sipped the lavender tea. "You know, Mordecai," she said after a few sips, "that cigar smoke is really making my tea taste awful." Emma offered Mordecai a small dish. She was losing her patience with the rude little man. "Now."

Mordecai begrudgingly tapped the fire out of his cigar.

"Please go on," Emma said as she made notes to share with Constantine. She sketched out an interior design for the Lavender Tea Room based upon Mordecai's descriptions.

Estelle watched Emma draw. "You know, Emma Bean, you are very good."

"I guess agriculture and art did come in handy after all," Emma said quietly.

"Odd combination, *non?*" Estelle said.

"Odd combination, yes." Emma said.

"The sketches of zee restaurant are exactly what we have in our minds. Oh, and did you know that Mordecai has a lavender sorbet recipe that goes perfect with zee lavender tea?"

Mordecai seemed suddenly distracted. "Estelle, why don't you make me another cup of lavender tea? Emma, would you mind if I use the washroom?"

Emma didn't even bother to look up at Mordecai but kept working at her sketches of the restaurant. "Upstairs at the end of the hall."

"HE'S A FREAK."

"Well, there's something creepy about both of them." Katie emptied the briefcase. The red book, the brown envelope with the secret opera score, the old music pieces and a calligraphy pen. *Hide the music.* Hide the music? Katie thought. Why? I trust Amanda and Evan completely. *Hide the music.* " I don't need to hide the music," Katie said out loud.

"Music?" The sudden presence of Mordecai W. Nightshade brought a kind of darkness into the room. "Did you say music?" He slithered toward the threesome like a juicy slug.

"Did you want something, Mr. Nightshade?" Katie said as she quickly slid the brown envelope back into the briefcase.

"Well, yes," Mordecai said. "The medicine chest is um...the Chinese box is of interest to me. I just wanted to take a quick look, if you don't mind." He took his gaze away from the briefcase, and directed it toward Amanda.

Amanda bristled. "Uh, yeah. Sure."

"Mmmm," Mordecai said. He touched the wood, then tried to cup the scent to his nose, as if trying to conjure a spirit from it. Then he leaned over and licked it.

Amanda glanced at Evan in a moment of mutual disgust.

"Subtle, yet definite – foxglove. Used for heart problems. Monkshood, used as a painkiller in Asia." Mordecai's left eyebrow shot upward. "Among other things."

"You have an unusual skill, Mr. Nightshade," said Evan. He wanted to divert Mordecai from the medicine chest and somehow get him out the door. "Yeah, but we really need to get to our studying."

"Old briefcase," Mordecai swiveled his head toward Katie. He sniffed about. "A kind of mimosa was used at the tannery and also vegetables of some sort. What exactly is in that briefcase?"

Katie opened her mouth but then quickly shut it. *Katie be quiet. Katie be quiet.* "We're really busy, Mr. Nightshade. Could you leave?" Katie looked point-blank at Mordecai as he rose with control from his squatting position and pulled at his moustache and tugged at his ear. He retrieved a hanky from inside his jacket and wiped his sweaty forehead and then his entire head.

"Of course. So sorry to keep you from your homework." Mordecai stepped backwards toward the door. He scanned the layout of the room as he left.

"G-L-A-B-R-O-U-S," Evan whispered.

"Déjà vu," Katie responded.

"What?" Evan replied.

"Nothing," Katie said.

Chapter 17

LASAGNA ON THE HOUSE...

GRAEME NOBLE HUNCHED OVER THE MESS OF papers strewn across his desk, the notes he'd made regarding the break-in at the Bean home. He clicked quickly from web site to web site with his right hand while the glass marble with the flourish of red kept his left hand occupied. He wasn't having much luck finding information on music theft. What kind of person would steal music? he wondered.

He found nothing. Plenty on art theft, but nothing on music theft. Graeme clicked on a link called AMAZING STORIES OF STOLEN ART TREASURES and browsed. He was tired. It was so easy to go off on tangents on the Internet and simply waste time. The computer monitor lit up his face as he read aloud. "Stolen works of art such as a Van Gogh or a Vermeer are sometimes kept by thieves for their own private viewing."

Graeme clicked on another link to an article titled, SUSPECTS FLEE TO CANADA. He read: "Two Provençals suspected in the theft of a sixteenth-century map have slipped Interpol custody. The man and woman have been investigated before on art theft, but nothing was ever proven. The trail has become cold." Graeme yawned. The article reminded him of his old buddy at Interpol, William Makepeace. Graeme tapped away at his keyboard.

Hello Makepeace,

Just on the Net browsing and came upon an Interpol story. I thought about you. Do you know anything about music theft? I'm doing some investigating. Not finding much about music theft, but plenty about stolen art.

Sounds weird, but there's a couple of odd characters just moved into town from the south of France or something. I know this sounds far-fetched but thought of them immediately when I read about the sixteenth-century map you and your mates at Interpol were investigating...probably nothing.

Hey, you still got that blotchy border collie – what was her name, Spot? Yeah. Well, just thought I'd drop you a line, old pal.

Graeme Noble

Graeme hit the *send* button. He took off his reading glasses and tossed them gently onto his research papers. He pocketed the glass marble, then rose and stretched. He was hungry and in need of a break. The lasagna he'd ordered from Queenie's the other night hadn't exactly fulfilled his expectations. He wondered about the new restaurant in the Chanteclaire Hotel. What was it called now? He had heard rumour. Then it came to him: The Lavender Tea Room. The place had once been the head-quarters for a plot to topple Thailand's economy, under the name of The Tuscany – awesome lasagna. Before that it was The Baby Panda – great ginger beef, but part of a diamond smuggling ring with links to Africa.

He had solved both cases. Graeme Noble wondered how it was that these exotic criminals seemed to find their way to a sleepy prairie town like Chanteclaire and bury themselves into the mix. His stomach grumbled. It needed lasagna. He hoped that this time the restaurant management was on the up and up – and that they had a good lasagna dish on their menu.

CONSTANTINE SEEMED A JOVIAL BEAR of a man as he greeted Graeme in the lobby of Chanteclaire Hotel. "Good evening, Detective Noble. What brings you to our fine establishment tonight? I assure you, there is no international crime revolving around my restaurant this time around. The Lavender Tea Room is being run by respectable people. The IMF can rest assured."

"Don't worry, you're no longer under surveillance," Graeme responded.

"Then what?"

"Lasagna."

"Lasagna?"

"Yeah, is yer new restaurant open then, Glitch?" Graeme scratched at the back of his head and smiled a tired smile at Constantine. "My weakness – lasagna." Graeme pulled the marble out of his pocket and into an easy fist. That marble comforted him and would do until his stomach was filled with lasagna.

"Lasagna, huh?" Constantine patted Graeme on the back and sighed. "Come. There is lasagna on the menu, although the specialty will obviously be Provençal to reflect our planned lavender field."

"Southern France?"

"Yes. Are you familiar with that part of the world?"

"Only from what I've learned on the Internet tonight."

"Oh? Anything interesting?"

"Nope." Graeme was tight-lipped.

Constantine guided Graeme through the hallway to the back part of the hotel that overlooked the five-acre stretch of prairie. "The lavender farm will be situated right there." The large man waved his arms toward the picturesque lobby view. "It will wrap partially around the hotel and then tier down the coulee hills. Might even get us a few grazing lambs." Constantine slapped Graeme on the back with his large palm. "The restaurant is currently being decorated. At this time the chefs are catering to hotel patrons only – it's not open to the public yet, I'm afraid. But I'll get them to prepare you a lasagna. I'm sure they won't mind trying it out for you."

"Funny, lasagna doesn't sound French," said Graeme.

"I think they're experimenting with integrating some lamb meat into the sauce."

"Experimenting? Lamb? You shouldn't have told me that, Glitch."

"Nonsense. Be adventuresome, Detective Noble. A lasagna connoisseur such as yourself will be a great critic for the kitchen staff." Constantine smiled at Graeme with enthusiasm. "Game?"

Graeme was starving, and all he wanted was a good old-fashioned plate of lasagna with a side of garlic toast. Something predictable that would satisfy his stomach. "Yeah, I dunno, Glitch." Queenie's was sounding good to Graeme now.

"On the house. I would be insulted if you said no."

"Aw-right."

"Okay then," Constantine said. "The deal is that you give me a review on the lasagna dish. A candid review."

Graeme smiled graciously and nodded. "Deal."

"Interested in some lavender tea while you're waiting?" Constantine offered.

"Nah."

"Wait here," Constantine said and ducked behind the red velvet drapes.

Graeme's stomach growled. He glanced at his watch – seven o'clock. He thrust his hand into his pocket and found the marble.

At 7:35 Constantine reappeared with a steaming take-home container in hand. "It's hot! Be careful."

"Thanks, Glitch."

"My pleasure, Detective. And now, I must be off. Hotel matters to attend to. A crisis in the honeymoon suite. It appears there is a couple of feet of suds in the bathroom. Bubble bath in a whirlpool tub is not a good idea.

"Good evening. Let me know how the lasagna tastes." Constantine bustled away, yelling to the front desk, "Get out the mops!"

Graeme balanced the lasagna on his right palm while he tossed the marble from his pocket up in his left hand. He caught it like he always did. He was quite proud of his dexterity and thought he'd try the trick one more time. The second time around was not a charm and the marble fell to the hardwood hallway and rolled along beneath the red velvet curtain. He read the sign: *The Lavender Tea Room, Opening Soon.* Graeme stopped and considered leaving the marble where it had rolled, but it was his favourite. He looked around for any hotel staff – there were none to be seen.

It won't take me long to find it and be gone, thought Graeme, as he slipped behind the red velvet drapes. The lighting was dim, but he could still make things out. He followed the floral-patterened carpet and spotted his marble, so clear it looked like a droplet of pure rain, and perfectly round, with that little tapering red plume inside. Yup, he thought, I can't lose this one. He reached down to pick up the marble, then paused. He couldn't help it – he was curious about the place.

Graeme Noble felt around the wall near the doorway for a light switch and found it. *Click.* He gasped.

Chapter 18

DABS OF LAVENDER PAINT...

"I'm beginning to like zee Emma Bean, Mordecai," Estelle said as she tightened the cap on the bottle of essence of lavender and put it in the box with the sugar cubes. She watched Emma close the front door of the Bean home. "It was nice to meet Katie's friends, non? Zee Amanda and zee Evan."

"I couldn't care less about them, Estelle. I want that briefcase. That brat must keep it up in her bedroom."

Mordecai turned on the ignition of his Mercedes and pulled slowly away from the Bean house. He noticed how the canopy of trees hid the house completely from the view of the neighbours. He noticed how one of the old oaks arched near Katie's bedroom window.

"This is not a good idea, Mordecai," Estelle said as her jaw tightened. "This little plan of yours, to satisfy zee past regret."

"What past regret?"

"John Bean was a piano prodigy, a boy genius of music – and you were only the dabbler. Let the child have zee father's music. Get rid of all zat debris in your head, you don't need to satisfy zee ego." Estelle breathed in the lavender to try to ease the stress she was feeling. She was missing her little poodle.

"You talk of ego. Look what you did to the Lavender Tea Room!" Mordecai's voice was getting higher and his face and head were turning the colour of ruby-red grapefruit. "Oh no, zee Stradivarius," he mimicked.

"No one in this little hick town would know a Caravaggio or a Stradivarius if it bit them in the back end, anyway. You expect me to live in this place? I shall surely die of cultural deprivation. Why didn't you simply leave it the way I decorated it? Now I shall wither up and die," Estelle said. She was tired. Her accent had disappeared completely.

"You're being melodramatic. In any case, it's a good thing I went into quick action today. Your crazy idea of filling the Lavender Tea Room with our art! You could have landed us in jail!" Mordecai yelled.

"Now who's being melodramatic? Hm?"

Mordecai pulled up to the house on the hill and saw the little white poodle. Coco was lying along the back of the chesterfield, stretched out horizontally in the middle of the picture window.

"Shut the headlights off before they hurt poor little Coco's eyes."

Something in Mordecai finally snapped. He flashed on the high beams so that they pointed directly into the picture window, blinding the little poodle. Mordecai then honked the car horn with long and short bleats. Coco became a puffball of white, jumping high in the air, and then falling between the picture window and the chesterfield.

Sweat began to drip from Mordecai's forehead and his head glowed like a thermometer ready to burst. Then he sat quietly.

Estelle sat quietly too. She was unusually calm as she looked at Mordecai. "A moment of insanity?"

Mordecai nodded. "Quite. Forgive me, my love?"

Estelle nodded. "You're tired – painting all day, meeting all night." She reached out and rubbed at his face. "Look at you – paint on your face. Just like the old days, my pumpkin."

"You know, Estelle. I really enjoyed painting today. I miss the painting days. Remember? A Monet here, a Picasso there? We were masters of the Masters, weren't we?"

"Mordecai, you were better than the Old Masters. Not one of your paintings has even stirred suspicion to this point. That is proof of your genius."

"Shall we try it again?" Mordecai said in desperation.

"Your hands..." Estelle said. "A lifetime of piano playing and painting has destroyed your hands." Estelle noticed more dabs of pink and purple paint on Mordecai's wrists.

"Well then, this heist of John Bean's music will be the last."

"There – again with the word heist," Estelle sighed. She noticed her poodle had climbed back up on the sofa.

She rushed out of the car and ran to the door. "My baby, did Daddy hurt zee leetle Coco's eyes?"

♪ ♪ ♪

THE CHINOOK *found its way into the corner room through the west-facing window. The still life of rose petals and purple thistle blew off the table and across the hard-wood floor. The figure put the paintbrush in the jar of mud-died distilled water and then squatted to pick up the delicate blossoms. It was difficult, of course, to pick up the petals with those gnarled fingers. But the petals were replaced in a composition that was visually close to the first time the figure had arranged them. It wasn't necessary to recreate the still life anyway, since the painting was nearly done. Besides, the wind would just scream through that same crack again and blow them about.*

A touch of purple here and a dab of pink there. He then began to cut a tea bag shape around the little painting. Cut to the quick, snippety snip. The scissors were becoming diffi-cult to use around the tea bag corners and the fingers began to throb. But over the last several weeks, eleven tea bags had been meticulously painted, cut and filled. It had taken time, but it was worth it. The painted tea bags were beautiful miniature canvases. Just one more to paint. The figure swept the rose petals and thistle off the spotlighted table and replaced them with a new subject, lavandula angusti-folia – *lavender.*

Chapter 18

BROWSIN' THE WEB...

"Find anything?" Amanda asked. She licked the tip of her finger.

"Not much on Opal Witherspoon," Evan said, taking a break from the computer screen.

"Look, Pan, you shouldn't be tasting those weird concoctions in that medicine chest."

"Part of my report is on the taste of my great-grandpa's stash. It's an in-depth report, Noble."

"Do you wanna start growing horns?"

"No."

"Do you want your tongue to fall off?"

"No."

"Do you wanna die?"

"No."

"Then stop taste-testing the one-hundred-year-old monkey bones. I mean it."

"Yeah, I guess you're right for once, Noble." Amanda wiped her fingers on her jeans. "Well, did you find anything on Opal Witherspoon?"

"Nothing except her obituary from the *Chanteclaire Times*. There's something here on her husband's death, though, that's interesting. He was mountain climbing in Peru. It seems local guides found Elmer Witherspoon's body lying contorted at the edge of a crevasse, his ice pick pierced through his chest."

"Nice story, Noble."

"The report says he fell while crossing a pass on Alpamayo."

"Alpa-who-yo?"

Katie chewed on the tip of her pencil. "The old doctor was a mountain climber?"

"Yeah," said Evan. "And get this, he was on an expedition with his son. They found crampons clinging to the icy rock face, but his son's body was never found. The Peruvian police determined Charles Witherspoon had fallen into the crevasse and a rescue attempt was never made."

"Hey, how long are you going to be on the computer?" Amanda said impatiently. "I have to get on there and check out the medicinal value of the linden tree."

Evan printed off the Witherspoon information "Hang on a minute, will ya? Geez, have a little patience."

♪ ♪ ♪

I SAID, GET OUT OF MY HOUSE! *The wind screeched through the old building. All of a sudden he remembered the icy wind cutting to the bone during that climb along the pass in Peru.*

Over time, father and son had climbed nearly every mountain in the Rockies. They were experienced climbers. Meticulous climbers. But when they attempted the mountains of Peru, Elmer Witherspoon no longer had the same strength he'd had before. He wasn't as meticulous and he certainly didn't have the same kind of patience as he did when he was a practicing doctor. When the father and son attempted to cross the Alpamayo pass, a huge chunk of ice the size of a grain elevator broke loose at the top of the mountain. The authorities said avalanches were occurring more regularly — attributed the phenomenon to global warming. The father was taken down the sheer ledge by the train of ice, and when the son finally found him, Elmer Witherspoon was nearly dead. Nearly.

Patience, patience, and then cut to the quick, snippety snip. There was plenty of patience within. Once, a long time ago, Elmer Witherspoon had made his son sit in the corner for two full days scribbling out those little eighth notes, rests, and bass clefs. Recording those little musical pieces with that marker. Whole notes, sixteenths, half rests, and on and on. But the most challenging was the treble clef. The way it swirled like a backwards S and then swooped down into a loop. Patience was needed when drawing the treble clef.

Chapter 19

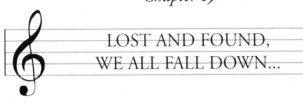

LOST AND FOUND,
WE ALL FALL DOWN...

IT WAS A COOL OCTOBER MORNING. KATIE COULD hear the usual morning sounds. There was a routine now. They had begun to settle into the town, into the house. But there was still that unspoken thing between her and her mom – they still never spoke of John Bean.

Katie played a little of "Emma's Song" on the piano. But she kept it quiet. Charlotte insisted it be a surprise until the university recital. The piece was so gentle it sounded like the piano was weeping. *Allegretto. Her father composed this piece in one night – he didn't sleep. The pillar candle flickered as he wrote the notes with a fury.*

"Are you ready, Katie?" Emma yelled from halfway up the stairs. "I have that meeting at eight o'clock this morning, so I'll drive you to school today."

"I'm ready."

"Are you playing the piano?"

"No," Katie lied. She reached into the old briefcase

to pull out her Baranski report and the little red book fell splayed to the floor.

"What is that? Where did you get that book?" Emma asked, scrambling down the rest of the stairs while hooking on her earrings. She reached down and picked up the book, recognized it as her husband's diary. Still walking, Emma read where it was opened.

> *I'm not much of a father. Not much of a husband. I haven't been able to support my own family with my music. This piano drowns me. But something is about to change. This opera. It's the best work I've ever done. I'm hopeful.*
>
> *Katie was sleeping. I snuck in to take a peek. Her wavy hair fell like a waterfall of fire on her pillow. She has these amazing fingers that are created perfectly for the piano. I know I will regret spending so much time with my work and not with Katie. She'd starve from lack of affection and attention if she had to rely on me. At least I can take solace in knowing she has Emma.*

Emma slowed her pace and began to cry. Her world suddenly stopped. The words hurt because she knew they hadn't been true since John's death. She knew that Katie *was* starving for affection and attention. Emma suddenly saw that she had been so devastated by John's death that she'd become blind to Katie's needs. The death, the move, the new job had essentially made her numb and only going through the motions of life. Only going through the motions of being a mother.

Emma bit her lip as she gazed at her daughter. "I'm so sorry." She reached for her, held her, ran her fingers through the fiery waterfall of hair that John described in his red book. "John is dead," she whispered. "Your father is dead."

Katie welcomed her mother's embrace.

"I'm sorry, Katie," Emma said. "I haven't been there for you, have I?"

"Where have you been, Mom?"

"Lost."

"Where?"

"I don't know. Somewhere out there."

"Me too," Katie admitted.

"Wanna be lost together, then?" Emma asked with a small smile.

Katie nodded and laughed through her tears. The tears felt so right. For the first time since her father's death, the tears felt right.

"You're late for school."

"You're late for work."

"Shall we both skip?" Emma said, wiping her tears.

Katie nodded, then paused. "Wait a minute, Mom. What about your meeting? You have a presentation to Uncle Connie and his staff this morning, remember? You've got to show them the harvesting proposal and that steam distiller. Present all your weird lavender ideas."

"They're not weird." Emma looked at her portfolio and the sketches she'd worked so hard on.

"C'mon, Mom, your job is weird. The people you work with are weird. Lavender on oatmeal? Weird. But you've worked so hard. Why don't you go to the hotel, make the presentation, and then come home? Really, I'll be fine. I'll just take a bath while you're gone."

"When did you grow up, Katie? Have I been so blind and selfish that I've missed it?"

"Well, basically, *yeah,* Mom." Katie smiled.

Emma gave her a hug. "I'll make it quick, okay? Then I'll come right back."

"We're two delinquents," Katie said with a soft giggle.

"Yup," Emma smiled. "I'll be home in a moment. We can heat up that leftover lasagna for breakfast."

"Aw, Mom, do we have to?" Katie laughed at her mom's obsession with lasagna.

"The truth is, lasagna is the remedy for all ailments, not lavender. Didn't you know that?" Emma smiled as she shut the door. The sound of her footsteps faded down the porch stairs.

Katie went upstairs to soak in the bathtub. She wanted a very long hot soak, and she even considered trying her mom's experimental lavender soap.

EIGHT O'CLOCK and the Bean neighbourhood seemed unusually quiet. The school bus had passed through. There was no usual sound of wind in the leaves. But there *was* something else rustling the leaves.

"Are you crazy?" Estelle looked up at the second-story window and the old oak that hung over the roof.

The neighbourhood was so thick with ancient oaks you could hold a three-ring circus in the backyard and no one would know. "You're not young anymore," she said. "You'll fall and kill yourself if you try to climb zee tree. Why don't we just go through zee doors or through a main floor window and make it easy?"

Mordecai tugged his gloves on so they were snug. "This may very well be my last heist, Estelle, and I want it to be a classic. The Bean girl is at school and Emma is at the hotel making a presentation to Constantine and the hotel staff. I have plenty of time to make this heist a work of real art thievery."

"Fine, fine," sighed Estelle. "But you are not stealing a work of art. There is a difference between zee master painting and zee kindergarten finger-painting."

Mordecai sneered at Estelle. "You just don't understand music." He began to climb. "As soon as I find John Bean's briefcase, I'll drop it over the eavestrough for you to catch. I can do this with my eyes closed. It's a foolproof plan."

"*Fool* being zee appropriate word." Estelle watched as Mordecai tried to shimmy across one of the thick limbs of the tree. The limb tapered off near the roofline and that is where it gave way to Mordecai's weight. He fell to the ground with a hard thud.

He looked sheepishly up at Estelle. "I seemed to have misjudged the hardiness of this tree. As you can see, all the trees in this neighbourhood are rather old, and this one is no exception. Weak substructures all of them. Dutch elm disease, no doubt."

"These are oak."

"Whatever."

"Perhaps you are simply too old and overweight to be climbing zee trees, Mordecai," Estelle said.

"I've climbed many a tree in my day, Estelle. Many a mountain." Mordecai began his ascent once again. This time he climbed for the next limb that gave access to the roof, which was a little bit higher. He made it to the roof, gave Estelle a haughty sneer and lost his footing. The sound of his body made a crack in addition to a thud as he hit the ground again. He got up more slowly this time around and brushed his backside off. "Shall we?" he said, waving a lock pick in the air. He led Estelle to the front door of the Bean house.

Chapter 20

HARD EVIDENCE...

"Hello, Mrs. Bean," Graeme Noble said. He caught up with Emma as she was rushing out the double glass doors of the Chanteclaire Hotel. She had managed to wrap up the presentation in an hour and a half. It was 9:30.

"Detective Noble," she said with a smile. "Hotel business?"

"Nope, I'm here off-duty on food critic business," Graeme laughed. "I promised Glitch a review on a meal that the Lavender Tea Room made me the other night. Just dropped a note off for him."

"Food any good?" Emma asked with a smile.

"Afraid not. Some foods shouldn't be lavenderized."

Emma laughed as she rummaged her purse for car keys. "Any more clues on the break-in at our house?"

"I'm piecing some things together. Perhaps you'd like to hear about it. Would you like a coffee?" Graeme breathed in the lavender fragrance that enveloped Emma. "I'm on foot. We could walk to the..."

"My daughter Katie and I are going to spend the morning together," Emma said. "We're playing hooky."

"Oh, something I should be investigating perhaps, eh? Playing hooky is a felony in Chanteclaire." He laughed a little and held the marble Evan had given him in the palm of his hand. "I wouldn't want to intrude on your mother-daughter time together, but this may be something that concerns you and the theft from your home, anyway."

"Oh, I see." Emma got into her car. "Come along with me and we can talk on the way to my house. Katie won't mind if you join us for brunch."

"Well, maybe for a bit," Graeme responded. "But only for a bit. It's your hooky time together, after all." He laughed.

"We're having lasagna," she added.

"For breakfast?"

"Anything wrong with that?

"Nope."

"Then get in."

Graeme examined the passenger side door. "Quite the dent ya got here on the passenger side door."

"See that tree over there?"

"Yeah."

"I hit it on the first day of work."

"Ah. I see." Graeme swung the passenger side seat belt over his shoulder, locked himself in. "Now, I heard you were working with the two from France," he said, as he double-checked the seat belt.

"Yes. Mordecai W. Nightshade and Estelle Michelle

are managing the Lavender Tea Room while I'm working on the lavender farm plans."

"You know, I had a sneak peek at the Lavender Tea Room. It's really something."

"Yes, all those paintings of the Masters behind that red velvet curtain. I mean, they were spectacular reproductions, but it was all a bit dark for my taste," Emma said.

"Paintings?" Graeme stared at Emma while she drove. "Dark? I saw nothin' of the sort. What I saw was the most ghastly room I've ever laid eyes on. Bright purple and pink lavender fields painted on the walls. It made me gasp in horror. But you say they had it decorated with some reproductions of the Old Masters prior to that?"

"Mordecai was annoyed with Estelle for putting them up. He wanted a fresher look. I guess he must have redecorated the restaurant in a lavender theme since I last saw it. Prior to that, there was a Van Gogh, Vermeer, Rembrandt...even an antique map of some kind."

"Tell me more," said Graeme.

KATIE FELT REFRESHED as she combed out her wet hair. A bubble bath always made her feel good. She looked at her fingers. They were all prune-like from her soak. She smelled her pajamas and suspected Emma of spritzing the flannel top and bottom with the lavender water. *Katie, be quiet. Katie, be quiet.* Did she hear something? She held the comb tight in her hand, looked over her shoulder and then back to the mirror. There behind her were Mordecai and Estelle.

"I've been investigating Nightshade and his partner Estelle Michelle since they arrived in Chante-claire. I have some serious suspicions about them. This just adds to them."

"What kind of suspicions?" Emma was terrified. "I've had them in my home a few times. Is there any danger to myself or to Katie?"

"I don't think so. If this is the couple I think they are, all they're interested in is high-end art. And I mean really high-end art. Remember those paintings in the Lavender Tea Room?"

"You mean those were originals?" Emma's car began to smoke a bit from under the hood, and it slowed down about a block down from her house, right in front of a beautiful hedge woven with blue morning glories. "I've been meaning to get that looked at," Emma said as the sputtering car came to a complete stop. "We'll have to walk."

Dusty Miller Drive was quiet. Quiet as dust.

"Interpol is looking for a couple of art thieves who'd been painting Old Master's works. I guess these artists were really good at reproduction. They would steal the originals and leave their fakes. It was only recently that the fakes were discovered."

"Clever. Too clever. This can't be Mordecai and Estelle. They're much too old."

"Yeah, they're old now, but these art crimes may have happened decades ago."

"Perhaps when they were in art school," Emma said, recalling their first meeting.

"Of course this is all speculation," Graeme said. "I mean, they could be just a couple from France starting a new life in Chanteclaire. But..."

"So why don't you just take them in for questioning?" Emma said as they walked up the porch.

"Well, I need some hard evidence," Graeme said as the front door to the Bean house swung open. "I can't do anything without some real hard..."

Estelle Michelle's mouth dropped. She was holding the vegetable-tanned briefcase. Mordecai W. Nightshade froze in the act of wrapping Katie to a kitchen chair with duct tape. They were as stiff as statues before Emma and Graeme.

"...evidence," Graeme said.

Chapter 21

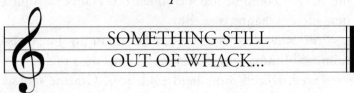

THE COMMOTION IN THE LIBRARY DIED DOWN AS Mrs. Zook guided Eugene Snycer to Principal Payne's office once again.

"So once Dad got his computer fixed, he discovered an e-mail from his buddy, Makepeace, at Interpol. Attached to the letter were photos of Mordecai and Estelle. It seems they'd been searching for them for a while. And get this. Mordecai had a full head of hair!"

"You mean they didn't 'fight or flight?'" Amanda said, while admiring the mark of ninety-eight per cent that Mr. Baranski had given her Chinese medicine presentation.

Katie rubbed her mouth with her fingers. It still hurt a bit from the duct tape. "Mr. Noble said Mordecai and Estelle were genius thieves in their day, but their day was a long, long time ago. Besides, I doubt Estelle could run very far in those stilettos."

"Ya know," Evan looked a little perplexed, "there is still something not quite right here. I just know it."

"The tea," Katie responded.

"Yeah, what about the tea that seems to show up in all these deaths?" Evan asked. "The police caught Mordecai and Estelle and recovered all that stolen art. Now they're investigating the possible tie-in of the Opal and Elmer Witherspoon deaths and that of your dad. They suspect Mordecai and Estelle had a hand in those cases too, but something still seems out of whack."

"Put it to rest. The police caught the bad guys. End of story," Amanda said.

"Yeah, I guess you're right." Katie forced a smile. "I just thought we were on to something else with my father's death. I thought it was leading in another direction."

"So, changing the subject, when is that concert you're performing in – the university one? Evan and I want to come and watch you play the piano."

"Yeah, I finally get a date with Amanda Pan." Evan pushed up his glasses and smiled.

Both Katie and Amanda ignored that comment as they walked down the Grade Eight wing toward the cafeteria.

"Charlotte hasn't said exactly what the date is. She's only said it's the annual university spring concert. I'll ask her this afternoon. I'm going there for another practice."

"Maybe my mom will know," said Amanda. "She works in the art gallery at the university. Yeah, I'm sure she'll know."

"Geez, Bean," Evan said as he slid into their usual places in the cafeteria. "How'd ya get so lucky as to meet a music professor who's willing ta put up with you for no charge at all? And serves you hot apple pie with rum sauce? That's my favourite, ya know. Maybe I could crash one of your piano lessons, huh?"

Once again Katie and Amanda ignored Evan.

Chapter 22

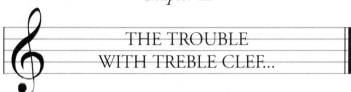

THE TROUBLE
WITH TREBLE CLEF...

KATIE FELT THE HEAVINESS OF THE BRIEFCASE AS IT swung to the rhythm of her steps. The afternoon had a bit of a chill to it, so she clutched her jacket collar close to her neck. She saw the blue morning glories along Charlotte's picket fence and deadheaded a few as she had seen Charlotte do. The spring-loaded gate clattered behind as Katie walked along the sidewalk to Charlotte's partially enclosed veranda. Stargazer lilies arched toward the midday sun. Katie could smell the aroma of apples and cinnamon at the screen door and her mouth watered with anticipation.

"Come on in," Charlotte called in response to the chime of the doorbell. She poked her head around from the kitchen, blue eyes contrasting with pale white skin and a haphazard flock of musty-brown curls. She smiled. "G-go ahead with your piano practice. I'm j-just finishing up the rum sauce."

Katie slipped off her shoes and felt the hardwood against her stocking feet.

"Mmmmm, smells good in here, Charlotte."

Katie sat on the piano bench and laid the briefcase beside her. She shuffled through the sheet music, found "Emma's Song" and spread it in front of her like a butterfly. She was eager to play today.

"Very w-well d-done." Charlotte said, listening to Katie play. The old woman sat in the corner where she usually marked her papers. "Have y-you d-done away with your backpack, then, or is this the c-cool way to carry books these days?" She gestured to the briefcase, then leaned back in her chair, slipped on her reading glasses and began to mark her papers as she always did when Katie was over. Katie figured she must surely be near the end of marking those papers.

Katie re-squared herself on the bench. "No, this is my father's old briefcase. I like to keep it with me these days." *Shhh, Katie, be quiet.*

"Oh, your father's, you say? So, this is *the* briefcase." Charlotte took off her reading glasses. She seemed fidgety – or she was simply being her absent-minded self. "John Bean's briefcase. What would John Bean's briefcase hold, then?" She pulled herself up out of the marking chair. "You know what?" Charlotte said. "Why don't we have our apple pie and rum sauce right now? Yes, let's. Some tea, too. This marking can wait."

Katie plunked on the F keys while she waited for Charlotte to serve up her delicious apple pie and rum sauce.

"Do you have a fascination with F keys, Katie Bean, or is that how you limber up your fingers?" Charlotte questioned from the kitchen. Her enunciation seemed crisp now and flawless, stuttering gone.

"Well, my dad's piano has a dead F key. I just like to hear one that works," Katie laughed. "That's all." Katie wandered over to the window that framed the old Chanteclaire schoolhouse and watched the grey clouds converge overhead. Tumbleweeds rolled over the coulees and across the open land in herds. She could feel a prickly coolness in the air. Then little slivers of rain came that sounded like they were running across the rooftop in staccato steps, then accelerating *a tempo*. A wind devil danced with the fallen leaves on the veranda and then unwound and invited itself through Charlotte's screen door, scattering her pile of marked papers all over the hardwood floor. One by one, the doors in the old Victorian house slammed shut from the gusts.

"Katie, could you shut the front door and the living room window?" Charlotte yelled, as the teakettle whistled above the commotion of wind and rain. "It seems we may have a hailstorm on its way."

Katie rushed to close the door as the wind fought her, then edged the wooden block out of the window and pulled it down snug to the sill. She raced around the house closing all the windows. Charlotte soon caught up with her. Katie had never been to the upper floor. In the master bedroom, the scent of lavender filled the air. A daisy pattern covered the shower curtains in the bathroom. In the spare room, a bay window overlooked the coulees and the ominous prairie sky. Katie lingered at the window of the art room, listening to the hail patter against the pane. The wind seemed to howl in the room.

"Come, let's go now," Charlotte urged. She seemed uneasy. "Our apple pie is waiting. This maelstrom will subside soon enough."

"Your stutter is gone." Katie said with curiosity. "Your bad leg? Is that gone, too?" For some reason Katie was getting a little nervous. Seeing Charlotte in a different way. *A little boy sitting in a corner, crying for hours at a time. He is surrounded by sheets of music and his knuckles are all red. A father yelling at the boy. Swooping and screaming like a wild wind and then hitting the boy's hands with a cane.* Katie backed away from Charlotte. *Katie, leave. Katie, run.*

"Well, my stutter comes and goes, Katie Bean," Charlotte said as she took off the oven gloves. Her fingers were thick and her knuckles as large as rocks.

"And your limp?"

"That seems to come and go as well." Charlotte smiled. But it was a different smile and a different face. It was eerie to Katie that an angelic face could so quickly turn glacial.

The doorbell rang. But it was hardly heard over the barrage of hail. It was ignored.

"You paint?" The room had been fitted out as an art studio.

Katie could hear a whisper. *Katie, be quiet. Run, Katie, run.* Katie took her eyes off Charlotte for a moment and saw pink rose petals scattered on the floor and lavender wilting on the small table. There was an easel with a large painting and then a sketchbook with some smaller studies of still life. "These are your subjects?"

"I do paint. It is my own private pleasure. Watercolour, you know. Because watercolours are gentle with my subjects. I take the smaller versions of the paintings and package them into tea bags. As gifts, you know." Charlotte pulled one of the drawers of her antique dresser open. It was filled with little bags of dried leaves and flowers and seeds.

In a way it reminded Katie of Amanda's medicine chest. Concoctions.

Charlotte closed the drawer quickly. "Oh dear, I'm losing my mind," she said nervously. "Now where did I put that?" She opened another drawer and found what she was looking for. "I was going to give this to you and your mother at a later date, but now that you have discovered my little passion..." Charlotte gave Katie a box filled with tea bags. "A gift from me to you." *Run, Katie, run.*

Katie pulled open the ribbon and lifted the lid. She pulled out one of the tea bags. There was a miniature painting of a Stargazer lily, outlined with pencil and a fine line of fucshia. The red bled into the orange that bled into the yellow, and large green leaves cupped the flower. A stem led down to the painted word, *Autumn.* Katie pulled the tea bag out completely and gasped when she saw the signature. It was a small treble clef in the bottom right-hand corner.

Katie looked up into the dresser mirror and saw the reflection of Charlotte standing at her side. Letters began to scrawl quickly across the mirror. *He's trying to kill me* arched above Charlotte's reflection. The same scribble that appeared on the brown envelope from her father's briefcase. Charlotte's hair was different. It looked like it was falling off. *She's trying to kill me.* Then the S disappeared. *He's trying to kill me.*

The doorbell rang.

"Is there something wrong?" Charlotte's voice had an edge to it. "Don't you like the gift?"

"Um, no. I mean, yes." Katie slowly made her way to the art room door. She kept an eye on Charlotte as she went carefully down the stairs. *Get out of the house, Katie. Now. Get out now.*

"NO. YES. NO. YES." Charlotte breathed down Katie's neck as she followed her too closely down the stairs. Charlotte's voice was sounding lower and lower.

"I think it's time for me to go now, Charlotte." Katie gripped the box of teas so tightly that the box was beginning to collapse and some of the tea bags were falling out.

"No, it's not time yet, Katie Bean," Charlotte said as she blocked her way. "We haven't had our apple pie and you haven't had your piano practice."

Charlotte's marking papers were strewn all over. "Don't you want to pick up your student papers, Charlotte?" Katie said nervously. Perhaps if she could distract the old woman somehow, then she could escape.

"No, you pick them up and I'll watch," said Charlotte as her voice strained and a thin smile spread. She picked up her cane and whipped it down on the pillows of the marking chair, causing the dust to fly. "PICK THEM UP!"

Katie put the crumpled box of teas on the bottom step and began to gather the papers. As she crouched, she kept her eyes on Charlotte and her cane. Katie put the sheets on the pile with the rest of the pages and then noticed the top sheet. One singular sentence was handwritten over and over on that sheet. She picked it up and read.

Cut to the quick snippety snip. Cut to the quick snippety snip.

Katie went through the pile of sheets and they were all the same. For all this time, Charlotte hadn't been marking student papers, but going slowly mad – or madder. Katie threw the ream of sheets at Charlotte, grabbed her father's briefcase and ran toward the front door. It was locked. She fumbled with the old latch and managed to open it.

Charlotte swung her cane at the doorknob and connected with Katie's fingers. "No, you don't. You haven't finished your lesson yet," she hissed as her face contorted. "Sit down." She pointed her cane toward the piano bench. "I'll take that." Charlotte grabbed the briefcase.

The wind blew the interior door wide open as the hail pounded on the screen door making it shudder in the frame. The hail was the size of golf balls now. They bounced off the veranda, off the siding, off the roof. The house shook. Glass broke somewhere in the house.

Charlotte opened the briefcase and pulled out the brown envelope that held John Bean's opera. She pulled out the sheet music. It was as if the clouds opened up for the old woman at that very moment – her face glowed. She held the music in her arms close to her chest.

"Finally it's mine. It's all mine."

Katie got up slowly and crept toward the door.

"But you can't leave, Charles. Where are you going? You haven't finished your piano lesson yet." Charlotte's voice was gruff and her eyes were lifeless. "Play the *Moonlight Sonata* for your father, Charles." Charlotte grabbed her cane and pointed it to the piano bench. "PLAY, I SAID."

Katie began to play ever so softly. She could escape, she thought. But she didn't want to leave without her father's briefcase. She looked around for something to throw at Charlotte, to distract her.

"YOU AREN'T CONCENTRATING, CHARLES WITHER-SPOON." The cane came down on the piano like the crack of a whip. "GO TO YOUR CORNER."

Katie pushed the piano bench toward Charlotte and

reached for her father's briefcase. She slipped on some of the marking sheets and fell to the ground.

Charlotte raised the cane. "Charles, you have to learn to go to your corner when I tell you to. I'll have to teach you a lesson."

A hand came out of nowhere and clutched the cane mid-air.

"No, *you'll* have to learn to go to the corner." Emma swung with all her might and connected with Charlotte's nose. Charlotte fell into a heap in the corner of the living room. Her hair fell off in a mass beside her, revealing her true identity.

Familiar faces filled Katie's line of sight. She felt all the fear release in tears. Detective Noble was there with her mother, with Evan and Amanda right behind him.

"Charles Witherspoon, I presume," said Graeme Noble as he linked the police cuffs on the unconscious figure. "The son of Dr. Elmer and Opal Witherspoon." He phoned the Chanteclaire police station for backup. His voice faded into the background.

Emma knelt by Katie. "Are you all right?" Tears fell on the briefcase that Katie was clutching tightly. Emma looked her daughter over from head to toe, then saw that her red hands were bleeding slightly. She held Katie's bruised fingers to her mouth and kissed them gently.

"I'm fine, Mom. How did you know I was here? How did you find out about Charlotte, or Charles – whatever her name is?"

Amanda and Evan circled around Katie.

"I asked my mom about the spring concert at the University of Chanteclaire and she said there wasn't one. That's when I became suspicious. So I asked her about Professor Charlotte Winston. She hadn't heard of a Professor Charlotte Winston." Amanda helped Katie onto the couch.

"Ever since I've been working on that Baranski report on the Witherspoons, my dad has actually been listening to what I've uncovered."

"*We've* uncovered," Amanda corrected.

"He kinda put *our* discoveries together with his Witherspoon cold cases and it all came together like a puzzle." Evan sniffed at the air. "Is that apple pie and rum sauce?"

Graeme Noble stood over Charles Witherspoon like a hawk. "Looks like he's out."

Katie approached the unconscious man. She looked carefully at Charles's face and body. He had a slight, willowy build for a man. A sparse amount of snow-white hair. The makeup was smeared now, and without the scarves or wig that he usually wore, he did look like a man. Katie felt shivers run up and down her neck and back. She couldn't believe how he'd fooled her.

"I guess we discovered one other thing," Evan said with a laugh.

"What's that?" Graeme said.

Emma rubbed her fist. It felt like she had broken a few fingers.

"We discovered where Katie gets her solid right hook." Evan followed the scent of the apple pie to the kitchen.

Chapter 23

THEN THE SCRIBBLE FADED...

"YEAH, OPAL WITHERSPOON WAS POISONED SLOWLY by her son. Charles was apparently a tormented soul. He sent his mother all these packages of beautiful and irresistible teas, laced with poisonous herbs. Hideous concoctions. She died slowly – one comforting, lulling sip at a time, over the course of a year."

"Same with Dad?" Katie said softly.

"Same fate as your father, yes." Graeme nodded. He regretted starting the conversation, forgetting to shift gears from detective to dinner guest.

"Iced tea, anyone?" Emma said.

Evan's mouth was full of garlic bread as he waved his empty glass.

"What about Dr. Elmer Witherspoon?" Katie said.

"Ya into hearing all this? All this talk of death and murders and such?" Graeme gulped his iced tea and eyed Katie.

Katie pulled her flaming red hair back behind her shoulders into a ponytail and then mopped up some sauce with a slice of garlic bread. "I want to hear the truth, is all."

Graeme looked at Emma for approval.

She nodded.

Graeme swallowed his last bite of lasagna and wiped his mouth with his napkin. "The authorities believe that Elmer Witherspoon did eventually die from the fall in Peru."

"Eventually?" Emma said.

"Charles Witherspoon did nothing to save his father. He left the old doctor on the edge of the crevasse to die. Charles was a very troubled soul."

The foursome at the table grew quiet.

"Oh, one more thing," Graeme said with a smile. He reached into his leather jacket and handed some pages over to Katie. "It's 'The Wishing Well.' Found 'er during the investigation of Mordecai and Estelle's house."

A smile grew on Katie's face as she took the music from Graeme. "Mr. Noble, thank you. I don't know what else to say. I —"

"Katie, shh, be quiet." Graeme rose from the table. "You don't have to say anything. That smile's enough for me."

Emma walked Graeme to the door. "Thank you for everything." She was so very tired. "It hasn't been an easy time for Katie and me this last year. We've been struggling with our relationship and struggling with John's death."

"Things are bound to get better," Graeme said as he stopped at the bottom step of the porch. "Abby left Evan and I when he was just ten years old. It hurt for the longest time. I'm not going to lie – still does. But life just goes on, doesn't it?" The sun was falling behind the old Chanteclaire schoolhouse. "That old wreck can sure look amazin' at sunset."

"I heard it was haunted," Emma said with a smile.

Graeme laughed softly. "I'll have to investigate that."

"Do ya think they like each other?" Evan said as he watched his dad and Emma from behind the screen door.

Katie shrugged. "Too soon to tell. Did your dad ever find anyone after your mom?"

"Nah. Dad's always so wrapped up in his work," Evan said. "Besides, why would he need anyone else, when he's got me?"

"Ah, right. Good point." Katie smiled. She noticed the sadness in Evan all of a sudden. "You miss her?"

"Huh? Who?"

"Your mom."

"Nope. She left us. I don't miss her. Neither of us do." He was quiet for a time. "It's kinda weird, though," he said after a while. "Seeing my dad with your mom. He's real gentle." Evan smiled as he walked out of the Bean house. "G-E-N-T-L-E."

"You're annoying, Noble," Katie said.

"Yeah. See ya at school."

Katie heard her mom calling out a goodbye to Graeme and Evan. She set the music sheets up and began to play. The music soothed her. Then she realized something was different about the piano. She stopped, and then plunked away solely at the F key. It was perfect. There wasn't the usual dead thud. She continued to play "The Wishing Well."

"Sounds good," Emma said as she walked in the house.

"You got the piano fixed then?"

"Can't keep a piano around with a dead F key," Emma said with a smile.

Katie laughed and began to play again. She saw the words scrawl across the top of the sheet in her father's handwriting. *You have each other.* Then the scribble faded away. "Did you see that?"

"What?" asked Emma.

Another scribble appeared. *Shh...Katie, be quiet.* Then faded.

"Oh, nothing."

ACKNOWLEDGMENTS

I WISH TO THANK MY FAMILY AND FRIENDS FOR their constant support.

Many young people were interested in this story and gave some helpful advice during different stages of the writing process. I would like to express my gratitude in particular to Madison Craig, Adam Houtekamer, Jessica Jones, Brenden Lindgren, Jessica Meaker, Faith Metzger, Brett Tamayose and Taylor Novakowski.

Thanks also to the following who inspired me and kept my pen moving on the paper: Marty Baceda, Mark Campbell, Erv Fehr, Tracy Harvey, Kathy Knowles, Peter Lee, Natalie Lindgren, Ian McDonald, Elizabeth McLachlan, Shelley Metzger, Tavis and Tami Nickerson, Keith Novakowski, Blake Tamayose, Ward and Bruna Tamayose, Carmen Toth and Jo Wiktorski.

Thank you to Laura Peetoom for her creative input and technical expertise; to Deanna Oye for sharing her piano knowledge and discussion about the University of Lethbridge's Steinway piano acquisition; and to Alberta Agriculture for information on specialty crop growth in Southern Alberta.

A very special thank you to Barbara Sapergia of Coteau Books for her encouragement and generosity with her time.

ABOUT THE AUTHOR

DARCY TAMAYOSE was born in southern Alberta where she is a graphic designer and writer. *Katie Be Quiet* is her first foray into the world of children's fiction. Her debut novel, *Odori,* was published in the spring of 2007. She lives with her family in Lethbridge, Alberta.